The Time Rippers

Phil Moore

Cover Art by Phil Moore via Midjourney

Published by Virtual Worlds
www.virtualworlds.com.au

ISBN: 978-0-9756329-3-2

VIRTUAL WORLDS

Contents

CHAPTER 1
R.I.P Felix

It was the year 2100, but Gonville & Caius College of Cambridge University still looked as if it belonged in the 14th century, with its unyielding three-storied sandstone walls weeping with age and perseverance; so when the flying car, driven by someone who was clearly under the influence of some mind-altering and reflex-inhibiting substance, crashed into the historic façade of Porters Lodge as it tried to go the wrong way down Trinity Street, leaving a rather large gash in one corner of the building and scattering sandstone rubble all over the pavement three metres below, it might have appeared to the unwary time traveller somewhat anachronistic. The collision – quite literally – of old and new. Or, if you prefer, the inevitable consequence of an immovable object as met by the irresistible force of a drunk driver. Time, and the distance between different moments in time, matters little when confronting the capricious audacity of human overreach. But then, don't we all sometimes bite off more than we can chew?

Fortunately for the driver of said flying car, there was no-one to witness their transgression, being 3am on a Thursday morning, and time-travel didn't exist yet. Though that was to change within the hour, for in the student accommodation rooms on the third floor of the College, two ill-matched (and therefore lifelong) companion post-graduate students were working late on their makeshift contraption.

Chase Tomley was a skinny lad with thin-rimmed glasses and

unruly hair. He had two PhD's under his belt (Physics and Computer Science) and was working on his third (Quantum Engineering). He was a true genius, not that any of his professors recognised the extent of his gifts. Or, for that matter, any of the local female population. At twenty years of age, he was still a virgin. He consoled himself with the thought that if someone like Steven Hawking could be married twice, then there was no reason he would not eventually get laid.

Ronan Llewellyn-Pritchard, on the other hand, was Irish, and therefore had no trouble with the ladies. The fact that he was good-looking, was a natural leader, and was charming and self-centred to boot had nothing whatsoever to do with it of course; because when it came right down to it, he was not very smart. At least not in the way institutions like Cambridge valued. Indeed, even by the standards of the Irish secondary school system, Ronan was not considered to be particularly bright. He barely finished high school. Yet here he was, a graduate of Cambridge with a doctorate in genetic biology. Sometimes it helps to come from a wealthy family; and the new Llewellyn-Pritchard Bottlers (LPB) wing would almost certainly be a valuable addition to the University.

Despite their seeming differences, Chase and Ronan were the best of friends. Indeed, they were each other's only friend. Ronan had pissed off too many people, either by force of personality, occasional Northern Irish political tirades, or through resentments over his privileged background (his family was in glass, with most of their wealth coming from the manufacture of beer bottles). Chase, on the other hand, was a geek in a world of geeks. He knew more than anyone else, including the professors, but so far had been unable to prove it. He was, to everyone except his mother, a disappointment. Even his Post-Doc work was uninspired, though a handful of supportive professors clung to the hope he would one day do something great. Something Nobel worthy. Something that would attract funding for the college. That was the only reason he still had rooms and any kind of financial support. But most people had given up on him and just found him annoying and arrogant. Ronan didn't care about any of that, and Chase didn't care that everyone thought Ronan was a privileged Irish republican asshole. He made him laugh.

Plus, they both enjoyed a drink, which is what they were doing now in their bedroom laboratory. Drinking beer. Specifically, a craft IPA called *TimeWarp*. Ronan had become an aficionado of craft beers, talking about their 'nose' and aftertaste, about hops and colour and 'fruity' tones. Chase just liked getting drunk. It allowed his brain to slow down enough that he could conduct a somewhat normal conversation with anyone who was not at his level (and let's face it, there was no-one at his level). Of course, if he then tried to do that with a girl, whatever charm he might have had seemed to vanish in a fog of alcoholic absurdity.

Chase tried to focus – Ronan was telling one of his stories. 'What did you say? You pushed the button?'

'No, no, no – the monkey pushed the button,' Ronan insisted. 'I didn't touch it. So technically it was the monkey's fault. 'Course I got blamed for it. Bloody monkey played all innocent. Like it didn't know what I was talkin' about. Spoiled a whole week's worth of samples. Had to start over.'

'Was it a macaque?'

'Yeah, total fuckin' mess.'

'I mean the monkey. Was it a macaque?'

'Oh. No, a rhesus, I think. Pink face. Ugly motherfucker.'

'That's a macaque,' Chase corrected. 'Yeah, they're like that. Cheeky bastards. I prefer chimps.'

'I don't trust chimps.'

'Why not?'

'They look at me… like they think they're smarter than me. You know?' Ronan took a swig of his beer. 'They're a fuckin' chimp. They're not smarter than me. They didn't go to university. They didn't fuck Suzie Watson in high school. They don't even wear pants – unless, you know, it's like for a circus or somethin'. They're the ones in the cage. I'm the one wearing the lab coat. I'm the fuckin' human in this relationship. They're not smarter than me. So, they should stop lookin' at me like they are.'

'Yeah. Chimps are like that. They look at you.' Sometimes it was easier to just agree with Ronan than engage in debate. Life was too short. 'What's the time?'

'Oh, yeah.' Ronan checked the clock. 'Any minute now.'

'We better get back.'

'What's the point?' Ronan moaned. 'I mean, how many times have we done this now?'

'Five hundred and thirty-eight.'

'At least! It's a waste of time.'

Chase laughed, thinking Ronan was making a pun. He wasn't. They finished their beers and grabbed their helmets off the coffee table, which were just welding visors with strong purple UV protection on the eye-slits. As he always did when passing, Chase tapped for luck the laminated poster stuck to the wall – an invitation to the Time Travellers Reception, held by Steven Hawking on the 28th of June 2009. Of course, Hawking died in 2018 and Chase never got to meet his hero. But perhaps one day…

Chase followed Ronan into the bedroom which, despite the unmade bed shoved into one corner, had been repurposed as a science laboratory.

You are cordially invited to

A RECEPTION FOR

TIME TRAVELLERS

Hosted by

★ PROFESSOR ★

STEPHEN HAWKING

To be held in the past, at

THE UNIVERSITY OF CAMBRIDGE

Gonville & Caius College, Trinity Street, Cambridge

Location: 52° 12' 21" N, 0° 7' 4.7" E

12:00 UT 28 JUNE 2009

NO RSVP REQUIRED

'This was your idea,' Chase reminded Ronan.

'I thought it would be fun. This is just boring. I'm bored. Science is boring.'

'I don't think it's boring,' Chase offered steadily.

'That's cause you're a natural-born geek,' Ronan declared. 'You find boring stuff interesting. No offense.'

'None taken,' Chase said sincerely.

'You find shit like photosynthesis fascinating.'

'I do.'

'You're a freak. And I mean that as a compliment.'

'I know you do.' And he did.

Ronan paused and turned to confront Chase. 'You're my best friend, Chase. You know that?'

'Likewise.'

'We're partners – in the non-sexual, strictly platonic, professional sense of the word.'

'Of course.'

That *TimeWarp* beer was really kicking in.

'But I still think it's a waste of time,' Ronan said, his hand on Chase's shoulder.

Chase laughed again.

Ronan still didn't get it. 'What?'

'Nothing.'

They stopped in front of the contraption. It was large and unwieldy, dominating the room – all wires and fibre-optic cables, curly tubes and nitrogen-cooled pipes brought to the brink of absolute zero kelvin, LED displays with arcane text scrolling by too fast to read, and laser emitters that provided the pressures and temperatures required for breaking the laws of physics. In the centre of this chaotic mess of a science experiment was a transparent plastic cabinet the size of the proverbial breadbox. Currently empty.

The whole contraption looked like something out of a Terry Gilliam nightmare and sounded like a steampunk particle accelerator. It had no place being in a student dormitory on the third floor of Caius College. But what the Master didn't know wouldn't hurt them. Of course, they had tried to get funding and a lab through proper channels, but no-one took the idea seriously; so they decided to just do it on their own. It would be a lark. This was just the prototype, of course, with all its guts exposed; botched together over the course of

18-months of trial-and-error experiments. The final machine would look much slicker – once they had shown the world it was not a fantasy and they could get serious funding.

Chase checked the readouts on the naked LED screen as they flashed past. Intoxicated as he was, he was still able to keep up with the stream. All appeared nominal. Above this was a large digital clock running the countdown.

10...9...8...7...

'I prefer rats over monkeys,' Ronan said while they waited. 'Rats don't look at you.'

'Yes they do,' Chase argued. 'They've got those creepy fuckin' pink eyes.'

'Yeah. But it just *looks* like they're lookin' at you. They're all blind.'

6...

'No, they're not.'

'What?'

'Rats aren't blind.'

5...

'Then why are their eyes pink?'

'They're albino.'

4...

'Really?' Ronan was stunned. 'Fuck. Well, at least they're dumb.'

3...

'Unlike chimps and macaques.' Chase tried to sound reassuring.

2...

'Damn right.'

1...

The machine burst into life. Things rattled and hummed, flashed and sparked, as the energy of the contraption's jury-rigged fusion reactor intensified.

Chase and Ronan calmly put on their helmets – visors up.

The tension in the machine increased. It started to tremble violently, as if it would fly apart any second.

Unconcerned, the lads lowered their protective visors and watched. They had done this five hundred and thirty-eight times before.

A sudden, blinding flash of light emitted from the centre of the machine and a live rat appeared magically inside the box. A white rat with pink eyes. The machine abruptly fell still, with just the sound of crackling ice and vapour as parts of it either warmed or cooled, like a giant spacetime refrigerator taking a breath after a heavy workout.

The lads lifted their visors and looked at the rat, bemused.

'It's alive,' Ronan finally said.

'... Yeah.'

'That's never happened before.'

'... No.'

'What does that mean?'

'I don't know,' Chase answered honestly.

'Did something go wrong?'

'No...' Then the penny dropped. 'I think it worked.'

Ronan looked at Chase. Then back at the rat. Then back at Chase. 'What do you mean you think it worked? What worked?'

'I mean…' as a stupefied grin spread across Chase's face, 'I think it worked.'

Ronan also started to grin. 'No fuckin' way.'

'We just sent a rat back in time and brought it home – alive.

We did it. We've made a fuckin' time machine.'

'No fuckin' way!'

'Fuckin' way!'

The lads high-fived, their raised visors colliding in the process. Ronan removed his helmet and leant into the machine.

'What did you see, Felix?' Ronan asked the rat. 'What was it like livin' in the past?'

'Why must you always name them?'

Felix looked at Ronan intensely with its pink eyes. Ronan pulled away.

'What?' Chase asked.

'He's lookin' at me funny.'

'Maybe he doesn't like the name.'

'Felix is a perfectly good name for a rat.'

'He's probably just freaked out. After all, he's the first creature to ever travel through time.'

'Felix the Rat,' Ronan declared. 'World's first chrono-naught!'

The lads then celebrated in the way only English graduate students can – with a silly dance. That was, until Felix began to squeal and spasm in the throes of a violent epileptic fit.

Ronan was horrified. 'Felix? What's wrong?' He turned to Chase. 'What's happening?'

The tremors became increasingly ferocious until Felix *exploded*!

The lads recoiled. 'What the fuck!' Ronan screamed.

Every interior surface of the cabinet was dripping with Felix blood and bits.

Chase removed his helmet and solemnly held it to his heart in tribute. 'Farewell Felix. You did not die in vain.'

Ronan touched the cabinet tenderly, grief-stricken. '... Felix...' Ronan then noticed something inside the box. 'Chase. What's that?'

'What?'

'There's something in there.'

'Yeah, it's rat guts.' Chase did not form attachments with their test animals. He could do without the emotional trauma.

'No, there's something else.'

Chase leaned in to get a closer look. Through the haze of blood he saw a small glowing, swirling sphere inside the cabinet. A floating bubble of cosmic energy about the size of a golf ball. 'What the fuck is that?'

CHAPTER 2
What Did You Do?!

Meanwhile, in the year 2018, in New York City, Beth Finkle was dressed in one of her many smart buttoned-up tan pantsuits (because why give them the chance), as she prepared her morning shot of coffee with the satisfying aural blitz of a home espresso machine. The bean grinder alone was loud enough to wake up the dead, which it did, in the form of roommate Aliyah Alexander, who was again sleeping on the couch instead of in her room like a normal person.

Aliyah peered sleepily over the back of the couch, her tangle of black curly hair offset by her not quite so dark skin, which was offset by her two sizes too big, lime green, *Little Shop of Horrors* pyjamas. She groaned audibly.

'I see you didn't make it to bed last night,' Beth said once she'd finished grinding her beans.

'Do you always get up this early?' Aliyah croaked.

'Most people in New York do, you know,' Beth said. 'Those of us who have a job.'

Aliyah took no offence. It was a running gag between them that Beth was the organised, responsible one; and Aliyah the creative butterfly who would one day fulfill her true potential as a cultural icon. One day.

'And what does an actuary actually do?' Aliyah asked.

'I've told you this.'

'I know. I still don't get it.'

'I predict the future,' Beth told her plainly.

'You'd think the pay would be better if you could do that.'

'And what kept you up all night?' Beth asked, changing the subject.

'I went down a rabbit hole of bootleg shows again,' Aliyah explained. 'I started in the West End and ended up in Boston watching out of town tryouts of shows that will never make it onto a Broadway stage.'

'So … research.'

'What day is it?'

'Thursday.'

Aliyah stretched adorably. 'Ahh. I love Thursdays. Anything could happen on a Thursday. They're almost as good as Tuesdays.'

Beth stepped out from the apartment's kitchen nook, fresh coffee in hand, and stood over Aliyah heaped on the couch. 'You are so lucky,' she said without irony.

'I know. You wanna be me, don't you?'

'So much.'

'So do it!' Aliyah sat up, suddenly alert. 'Stay home. We can order pizza and binge the new season of *Outlander.*'

'Wish I could. Besides, don't you have a rehearsal this afternoon for your thing?'

'The Workshop, yeah.' Aliyah was unenthused.

'Is it not good?'

'It's okay, I guess.'

'What's it about?' Beth asked as she sipped her coffee.

'You know the movie: *The Time Machine*?'

'It was a book first.'

'Well, it's that.'

'Hasn't that been done?'

'Not as a musical...I think.' Aliyah wasn't sure.

'Good part?'

'Weena, the Eloi girl. She's the one the time traveller falls in love with.'

'It's a lead,' Beth said encouragingly.

'Yeah. But she's a bit of a wimp. I'm trying to convince them to make her more Xena, Warrior Princess.' Without rising from the couch Aliyah performed some impromptu Ninja moves to demonstrate. 'Have her punch out a few of those evil Morlocks. Give her some balls.'

'And maybe some agency beyond being a love interest,' Beth pointed out.

'Yeah. That too.'

Unlike Aliyah, Beth was not a musical theatre geek. She was a history geek. It had been her major at college and remained her passion as an amateur, though her other passion for maths and stats had become her profession. Beth liked the clarity of well-researched data, and the statistical challenge of predictive analysis. By contrast Theatre, or indeed anything to do with the arts, was too unpredictable. You'd have to be mad to try make a living at an industry so capricious. Aliyah was just the right kind of mad to make it work. Beth admired that about her, but she'd had enough of these conversations to know the obstacles.

'Are you getting paid?' Beth didn't like seeing Aliyah taken advantage of. And a bit of help with the rent on their upper west side New York apartment would also be appreciated.

'I'm co-producing, so of course I'm not getting paid. But it'll be worth it once we get it up.'

'Once you knock it into shape,' Beth said encouragingly,

echoing Aliyah's own words about previous efforts that never got off the ground.

'Precisely.'

'Is this with Owen and Clive again?'

'Yep. Another Clive-Owen spectacular.'

'You sure those two aren't English?'

'New England.'

'Not the same thing.'

'I could really go for an English guy.'

'It's the accent,' Beth agreed.

'Provided he wasn't a total wuss.'

Their conversations often went on strange tangents like this, especially when it came to men.

Aliyah mused aloud, 'If you could go back in time, where would you want to go?'

'Woodstock,' Beth said immediately.

'Really?! 'Aliyah was astonished. 'I would have thought something more…scientific.'

'It's one of the few times something that big had a genuinely positive effect on the world. At least for a while.'

'Yeah, that'd be cool. Woodstock.'

'What about you?'

Aliyah thought for a moment. 'Germany in the 1920's. You know, like in *Cabaret*. Looks like a really cool period.'

Aliyah's knowledge of history came mostly from the movies or musicals; though Beth had to admit the roaring 20's was a fun period – jazz, flappers, art deco, silent movies and post-war prosperity (before everything turned to shit again).

'Will you be home tonight?' Beth asked, pivoting.

Aliyah grinned. 'I'll bring the pizza.'

'You know it makes you fart.'

'So what? It's just us.'

Beth finished her coffee, left the cup on the table, and made for the door. 'Give my regards to off-off-Broadway.'

'It's all part of the master plan!' Aliyah declaimed as Beth closed the door behind her.

Aliyah groaned again and dragged herself to her feet. 'S'pose I better get dressed then.' She told herself, then smelled her armpit. 'Shower first.'

The theatre district of Manhattan was a great place to hang out. Aliyah liked to just wander the streets sometimes, look up at the theatre fronts, and dream. She couldn't afford to go to any of the shows, but she desperately wanted to be in one of them. Of all the Broadway theatres, only two actually fronted the street called Broadway – the Wintergarden and The Broadway Theatre. Most of the others were just round the corner on one of the side streets. There were forty-one official Broadway theatres in all, meaning they all had a seating capacity of 500 or more, and therefore shows in those theatres qualified for the *Tonys*. Off-Broadway was anything with a smaller capacity and were usually just a bit further away from the main Theatre District around Times Square. Off-Off-Broadway were venues that were smaller still, under 100 seats, and which tended to be down in Greenwich Village. Often, they were just a converted church, or the back of a coffee shop, or some room above a store, or in the back of a bookshop. Still, over the years even *Off-Off* had shed its avant-garde roots and gained some level of respectability. So, a new underground was emerging – something *off-off-off* – in Hell's Kitchen (at least it was still Manhattan), and this was where

Aliyah's show, the Clive-Owen spectacular *The Time Machine– The Musical,* was getting its first little run, in a converted 'Club' with a troubled history and sordid reputation, which Owen has somehow managed to fenagle for free, and which they had dubbed the 'Pagan Playhouse' as a nod to its dissident past. Assuming they could get the show to opening night.

Aliyah enjoyed the walk alongside the Hudson River, under the Joe DiMaggio highway and on down to 12th Avenue. It was a trek, but she got her steps in. Sometimes she would take the long way down Broadway to Lincoln Centre before turning west, just to bask in the history of the area. Despite their converted Club being a far cry from a true theatre, they were infusing it with the same spirit as all those other, bigger, historic venues. They were putting on a show!

'You know there's already been a musical based on *The Time Machine.*' This was what Aliyah heard as she walked into the *Playhouse.* Brad, the show's leading man, had a great voice, and he certainly looked the part, but could be a real buzzkill. One got the impression he wasn't truly committed to the venture and would have turned it down if he had *anything* better to do.

'There's been several,' responded Clive unfazed. 'The moment the book lapsed into public domain everyone jumped on it. Ours is but one among many.'

'Then why do it? Can't you come up with something … you know… *original*?'

'All the best shows are adaptations,' Owen suggested, equally unfazed. 'You know there are two *Phantoms*; and at least three *Frankensteins.* So what if there are other *Time Machines* out there. Ours will be the best!'

Aliyah smiled. This was why she liked these guys – they

were fearless. Clive wrote the words, Owen the music. Partners in both work and life.

Owen spotted Aliyah at the door and waved her over. 'Yoo Hoo! Here's our Weena,' then as an aside to Clive, 'I love saying that name.'

After the obligatory kisses and hugs, they got down to business. Owen was at the piano as Musical Director, while Clive sat front-and-centre facing the tiny stage as Director. The show featured an ensemble who collectively played both the Eloi and the Morlocks, with quick costume changes planned between scenes. On a bigger stage this might have been twenty people. Here they could only fit three, leaving barely enough room for the leads to perform 'downstage'. Indeed, the stage was just a few riser boxes with carpet offcuts stapled on top, and a canvas backdrop salvaged from some metal band that had broken up due to 'creative differences', and who were offloading their set pieces to anyone who would take them. The cryptic lettering of the band's incomprehensible name that was emblazoned on the canvas backdrop strangely lent itself to the post-apocalyptic paradise that was the world of their show – like alien graffiti scrawled on the side of a derelict building. That, along with some plastic vines and flowers draped over the scaffolding was the extent of their set so far.

Since Brad was having a moment because his voice wasn't warmed up yet, they began with Aliyah's Act One solo number where, shortly after being saved from drowning by the Time Traveller, Weena introduces him to her world. The ensemble, as fellow Eloi, joined in on the choruses and flitted about awkwardly upstage like hippies on a bad acid trip.

We are the Eloi
The people of this land
We live in the ruins of the past
It's a simple life
A happy life
Though we know it cannot last

We are the Eloi
The people of this land
We sleep under stars every night
We have no fear
We have no cares
And we have no way to fight

The number was still rough as guts, but the melody was sweet and gave Aliyah a chance to showcase her falsetto range. Which was fine for this early part of the show, but she really wanted something with belt in Act Two that showed her transformation from meek, mild Weena to amazon warrior Xena. Act Two needed a lot of work.

As Aliyah moved two steps downstage-centre (which was all the space allowed for) to sing the final chorus, she noticed a strange ball of 'something' floating directly in front of her. It vibrated in sympathy to her voice, its surface swirling with colourful musical patterns. Astonished, Aliyah stopped singing. The ball of energy calmed, though continued to pulse in rhythm to the piano, until Owen's fingers ground to a halt. 'What's wrong?'

The ball settled into a dormant state but remained floating in mid-air directly in front of Aliyah.

Clive chimed in: 'Aliyah...?'

Aliyah pointed at the golf-ball sized space-time anomaly

floating before her. 'Is this meant to be here?'

'What?'

Aliyah cautiously moved around the anomaly, checking it out on all sides. 'This bubble... thing. Is it a special effect or something?'

Clive stood and now saw what Aliyah was seeing. 'That's weird. I have no idea what that is. Owen?'

Owen shrugged. 'Never seen it before.'

Aliyah reached out with a finger to poke it.

'Don't touch it,' Clive warned.

'Why not?'

'It might be dangerous.'

'We don't know what *it* is,' Aliyah argued.

'Precisely.'

Aliyah poked it anyway. Her finger easily entered the floating ball of energy up to the first knuckle. She pulled her finger out – it was unharmed. The ball then swirled with colour and energy, growing in size. Aliyah and Clive stepped away, stunned. Everyone else watched with a mixture of awe and terror – not sure whether to flee, freeze, fight or fawn.

The thing grew as big as a melon before finally settling back into its dormant state.

Clive turned to Aliyah accusingly. 'What did you do!?'

CHAPTER 3
Domesday

'So you've made a time machine. Is that right?'

Chase and Ronan nodded sheepishly.

'In your bedroom.'

Nod.

Professor Alice Beauchamp, Director of Studies for the Physics Department of Cambridge University, sighed audibly. She was a stern, inscrutable, no bullshit kind of person who had worked her way up the academic ladder and was one of the leading computer science intellectuals in the world. Her specialty was artificial intelligence and its practical applications. She had already won a Turing Award and dozens of other medals and statuettes for her ground-breaking work in quantum cybernetics, all of which were meticulously displayed in the glass cabinet behind her. There was a particular space in the middle reserved for her Nobel, which was inevitably in her future. She was also quite young for someone in her position – Chase guessed mid-thirties, though she looked younger. He had something of a professional (and occasionally more primal) crush on her.

Chase and Ronan sat in two comfy old leather chairs across from the professor's enormous desk, surrounded by modern art and old varnished wood panelling. Strictly speaking she was Chase's supervisor, not Ronan's – he came from a different department –

and this was not the project Chase was supposed to be working on. Officially his post-doctorate was in developing AI systems for robotic sensors – sound, vision, touch and smell – and their application to autonomous extra-terrestrial explorer droids. The kind of stuff we send to Mars, Titan or Europa. Droids that would transmit sensory data, so someone back on earth could experience what it's like to really be there, without the inconvenience of a long space trip or suffocating to death in some poisonous alien atmosphere. That was the project for which he had received funding. That was the project he was supposed to be working on. Before this idea, the lads had pitched a biological matter transporter with temporal and geographical compensations that promised to convey objects from anywhere to anywhere else in the blink of an eye. It was ambitious, potentially ground-breaking, and too far-fetched to attract any serious funding. It had been deemed impractical. But they had gone ahead with it anyway, in their own time, with no direct funding, in their bedroom.

'Your original proposal was for a matter transporter,' Beauchamp said.

"It was,' Chase answered. 'It is.'

'We just decided to focus more on the … *temporal* side of things,' Ronan added.

In stark contrast to the old school décor of the rest of the office, Professor Beauchamp sat in a high-backed modern leather swivel chair wearing a simple but stylish red dress that was both professionally understated and sexy as hell. She tapped a pen nervously on the polished mahogany wood of her gigantic old desk as she considered whether or not to believe their story.

'A time machine,' she repeated thoughtfully while going

over the math in her head. 'And you think you may have ripped a hole in spacetime because your test animal – '

'Felix,' Ronan reminded her.

'… because Felix exploded upon return.'

The lads nodded sheepishly.

Ronan then performed a recreation of the event, wiggling his fingers to show the growing intensity of Felix's distress, and exploding his hands out for the final devastating moment – all with suitably grisly sound effects, which only served to underline his own grief at the loss.

Alice Beauchamp remained inscrutable. 'And now this … *anomaly,'* she continued pedantically, 'is getting bigger. Growing. And you're afraid it might engulf the entire university if left unchecked.'

'No,' Chase corrected. 'Universe. The entire universe.'

Beauchamp stopped tapping her pen momentarily … then started up again as she tried to do the math on that bombshell statement. After a few awkward seconds she stopped tapping once more, having come to a decision. 'All right then,' she said at last. 'Let's take a look, shall we?'

Professor Beauchamp, Chase and Ronan stood before the contraption. The sphere of faulty spacetime – the Anomaly – was now the size of a basketball and had completely engulfed the transparent box within which it had formed. Its surface swirled with latent energy and colour, like an oily slick trying to escape its own surface tension.

'Pretty,' Beauchamp said, transfixed by the phenomenon.

Chase didn't find it pretty. 'Any attempt to contain it just makes it bigger. Any attempt to analyse it just makes it bigger. In fact, anything we do – '

'– Just makes it bigger,' Beauchamp finished. 'I get it.' She leaned in for a closer look. 'It is curious.' She pulled the pen from her pocket (yes, her dress had pockets, she was a scientist after all) and slowly pushed the tip towards the Anomaly. It breached the surface easily.

…Nothing happened.

She pushed the pen in deeper. Once it was half immersed in the bubble the pen was suddenly *sucked* from her hand, vanishing into the sphere. Alice recoiled in surprise. The anomaly swirled actively and began to grow again, consuming the very machine that created it.

All three of them stepped away, watching it grow... and grow, as the Anomaly consumed everything in its wake. Finally, it stabilized at about two-meters diameter. A giant beautiful ball of mass-eating energy. The contraption that had spawned it was completely destroyed; indeed, a corner of Chase's bedroom has been consumed by the insatiable sphere.

'That was my favourite pen,' Alice Beauchamp said.

'How do we stop it?' Chase asked.

'I don't know,' she replied, then looked hard at the two lads. 'But you better come up with something pretty fuckin' quick before it eats the whole goddam planet!'

Meanwhile, in England, in the Middle Ages, in the year 1086 AD on a miserable, drizzly, Thursday afternoon, a young man by the name of Edmund Constable was walking up a dirt (or rather, mud) road, traveling from house to house, carrying a large book which was bound against the elements in thick leather wrappings.

Edmund had been tramping around the country like this for the better part of five months. His pale, skinny features and straggly hair betrayed the toll this mission had so far taken. He used to be plump and fair-haired, would drink wine each night with his evening meal as he flirted with the waitresses at his local tavern, and even got the occasional tumble when he could convince one or other of them to visit with him in his chambers near Alders-Gate in the north of London. As a servant of King William, and despite being a mere clerk, he lived a privileged life within the palace grounds. The brutal years of the Norman conquests were twenty years past and Edmund had been a child when all that happened. These days things were more civilized, and people were rarely killed for no reason. Still, as a servant of the King, he was obliged to do whatever the King commanded, even if it meant spending a year on the road collating an audit of the King's subjects. He was not the only one of course, there were many scribes like him on this grand census, but somehow Edmund got stuck with the sprawling county of York in the north of the land, where his threadbare tunic barely kept out the cold, despite a pelisson of fox-fur; and his woollen drawers proved less than adequate in keeping his vitals warm and dry.

To make matters worse, the local peasants were ill-informed about the King and his reign; though they well remembered the famine caused by William's suppression of an uprising a generation earlier. Nevertheless, Edmund was on a mission, and he intended to fulfill it to the best of his ability, so that when he returned the King would show favour, and perhaps allow him to marry one of the finer ladies of the court. Preferably someone with a healthy dowry and inheritance. Assuming, of course, he ever got to meet the King in person, who spent most of his time these days across the channel in Normandy.

Edmund pulled his tunic tightly around him as a chill wind came up the hill and hit him in the face. In court the tunic was the height of fashion – burgundy coloured with an embroidered design sewn into the front and fur around the collar. But out here in the wilds it proved an inadequate shield against the elements as the heavy cloth became saturated and made him stick out like an overripe plum.

Edmund quickened his pace and approached a farmhouse, knocking firmly at the crooked door. The man who answered was wizened by hard labour and meagre food, but was nevertheless unnaturally tall and robust. Why was it that everyone in York was bigger than him? Edmund wondered. The man wore the drab grey linen of all peasants, though his leather boots were in reasonably good condition. Edmund was jealous, as his own boots had holes in them. The man looked about fifty years old but was probably closer to thirty. Over the months Edmund had become good at guessing people's ages. Everyone in these parts was at least ten years younger than they appeared. It was a hard life.

The man glared at Edmund. 'Yeah?'

Edmund had also become used to the surly mistrust of the York natives. He found the best counter was a cheerful rejoinder. 'Good day to you, sir,' he smiled and doffed his sodden cap. 'My name is Edmund Constable. I am in the service of the King and have come here so that I may take a census for His Majesty. And you are – ?'

'A what?'

'A census. An account of all your possessions … for the official record. And your name is – ?'

'What King?'

'King William? …William the Conqueror? …Victor at the Battle of Hastings? …The Duke of Normandy?'

The man clearly didn't know who Edmund was talking about, so he resorted once more to the King's better-known moniker in these parts. 'William the Bastard?'

'Oh! Him.' The man spat at the ground. 'So what does *he* want?'

'I have been ordered to travel the land and take an account of all the King's possessions and holding in these parts.' The man glared at him again. 'It's an official record. The first of its kind ever done. You should be honoured to be included in it.'

The man was unconvinced. 'Yeah... We don't have that much.'

'Even so. It is my responsibility to write an account of all you possess, no matter how meagre.' The man didn't move. 'Or would you prefer I returned with soldiers to help me conduct my survey?'

This threat usually worked, not that Edmund had any soldiers at his disposal that he could call upon. The closest barracks was hundreds of miles and twelve days march away. But the man huffed and grumbled and opened the door to admit the unwelcome guest.

'Thank you, good sir. And what is your name?'

'John.'

Another John, Edmund thought. 'Thank you, John.'

Inside, Edmund found a squalid little house to match its squalid exterior. Made of solid wood beams with a vaulted thatch roof, there was an open fireplace in the centre of the room, straw beds against the walls, and an uneven table with two equally ill-made chairs set to one side. When he began this mission Edmund had been shocked at how these people lived, but after so many months he now took it for granted and was not at all surprised when he saw the man's wife and five children cowering in the shadows in a corner of the hovel. For some reason everyone was either deeply suspicious or plain terrified of him.

Edmund hefted the book onto the wobbly table. He untied the wrappings and gently opened the volume, flipping to the page of the ledger he was presently up to. He opened the pouch hanging by his hip and from it produced an ink bottle and quill. He placed the bottle on the unsteady table and uncorked it, then sharpened the quill with a small blade. As he did all this the family just watched in fascination. They had never seen such implements.

Ready, Edmund turned to his host. 'This is your family?'

'Hmm.'

'What is your wife's name?'

John looked at his wife, suddenly fearful she might be taken from him.

'All I want is her name,' Edmund reassured. 'Nothing more.'

'...Isabella,' John said at last.

Edmund nodded and jotted the names into the book. Strictly speaking the wife didn't matter, but he felt it only polite to include a spouse in the record if there was one. The children, on the other hand, would likely die before long, so why waste the ink. 'And you are tenant farmers under the rule of Richmond, yes?'

John shuddered, which Edmund took as confirmation.

'Yes,' Edmund said for the record, meaning they were serfs beholden to the lord of Richmond Castle who ruled over these parts, and who was the real subject of the audit. 'Do you have anything of value?'

'Like what?'

'Coin or gold?'

31

John laughed out loud. 'What do you take me for? A bloody noble?'

Edmund scowled at him. He knew they would have no valuables, but he had to ask. 'Do you have livestock?'

John's smile vanished. 'Out back.'

Edmund picked the book off the table and cradled it in his arm. 'Show me.'

John led the clerk outside and showed him a sty with a few pigs – hairy, spiky beasts that snorted and growled at their approach – and a coop with several chickens. Edmund counted the animals and added this number to his record in the book. 'What about that?' he asked.

John looked to where Edmund was pointing, head askew as he considered the curious giant ball of swirling light floating just above the ground. 'Never seen it before.'

'Oh, come now. It's on your land. What is it?'

'No idea.'

'How much is it worth?'

'How the hell would I know?'

'There's no need for blasphemy,' Edmund chastised. 'How am I to record this if I don't know what it is?'

John just looked at him blankly.

Ignorant peasant. Edmund shook his head with irritation and approached the ball. It was as big as a horse or a cow, if there had been a horse or cow on hand to compare it against. He reached out and poked it. His hand went clean through. Edmund quickly pulled his hand out. No harm done.

'I wouldn't be doin' that if I was you,' John warned as he stepped away.

Edmund tried again, reaching in a bit deeper this time. He

turned to John, arm still inside the sphere. 'Are you sure you don't know what –!' The anomaly *sucked* Edmund in. As he disappeared inside the swirling mass, the volume he was holding dropped to the ground revealing its cover – *The Domesday Book.*

John looked at the book, then back up at the colourful swirling ball as it doubled in size before his eyes.

John turned on his heel and ran back inside, calling to his wife: 'Issy? We're moving!'

CHAPTER 4
Message in a Bottle

Chase and Ronan stood guard over their growing Anomaly from the living room, each with a craft beer in their hand and a dour expression on their face. The Anomaly was now four meters in diameter and had eaten into the floors above and below the room. It had also consumed Chase's bed. Hazard tape had been placed across the doorway with a sign reading: *Do not feed the Anomaly*.

'I don't want the universe to end,' Ronan moaned drunkenly. 'I live in the universe.'

'We all do, Ronan.'

'So how do we stop this thing from growing?'

'We need to understand exactly what went wrong so we can reverse it somehow.'

'It's pretty clear what went wrong – we ripped a hole in spacetime.' Then, thinking out loud, Ronan added: 'And what do you do with a rip? You sew it up.'

'Okay. So how do we 'sew' up a tear in spacetime?'

'Gravity?'

Chase did the math in his head. 'You'd need the gravitational force of a black hole.'

'Oh. Never mind, then.'

'No, it was a good idea,' Chase said, and meant it. 'We just have to come up with something more ... practical'.

The Anomaly shivered and expanded by another meter. The

lads watched anxiously. Once it had settled down again, Ronan took another swig, finishing his beer. 'Why does it keep doing that? We're not touching it.'

'No. But maybe someone else is.'

Ronan looked about. 'Who?'

Chase explained. 'It's a rip in spacetime, right? A portal. So maybe it's showing up in another time, and people are finding it. Poking it. Throwing things at it.'

'Why would they do that?'

'We did that! It's human nature. People are gonna keep poking this thing till it engulfs the whole planet.'

'Well, we gotta stop 'em. How do we stop 'em?!' Ronan was railing against stupid humans and their stupid compulsion to poke things they didn't understand. 'How do we tell 'em to leave it alone?'

'We need to communicate with them somehow.'

'Like a message in a bottle.'

'Yeah.' This was why Chase liked Ronan so much, people assumed he was not smart, but his naïve genius was in lateral thinking and metaphor. He was the Jobs to Chase's Wozniak. 'If we could find a way of sending a radio transmission that could latch onto a suitable playback device on the other side; or better yet a pure audio signal ... provided waves of air-pressure will transmit into and out of this thing – it might be a vacuum inside after all – so we'll need a medium, and a transmission device of some kind.'

'Like a message in a bottle.' Ronan raises his empty beer bottle to illustrate.

Chase smiled – sometimes the metaphor was not a metaphor at all. Chase grabbed a notepad, wrote their message, rolled up the scrap of paper and stuffed it inside the empty bottle. He offered the bottle to Ronan. 'You do it.'

'Why me?'

'I throw like a girl.'

'True.' Ronan took the bottle and prepared to pitch it into the Anomaly, then hesitated. 'You sure about this?'

'No.'

'Okay. Just checking.' Ronan hurled the bottle into the Anomaly. It tumbled inside and vanished –

– to fly out of the Anomaly which now dominated the tiny stage of the Pagan Playhouse. The bottle spun end-over-end like a thighbone as it flew over the empty seating before landing with a clatter at the back of the theatre. It then rolled down the aisle back towards the stage where Aliyah snatched it up. She kept a keen eye on the Anomaly behind her as it once again swirled and swelled by another few feet. One of the show's braver ensemble members was filming from the back of the theatre with a smartphone, but the place was otherwise empty, everyone else having fled the scene.

Owen poked his head in from the back door. 'Aliyah! What are you doing? Leave that thing alone. You'll just make it worse.' Then he saw the Anomaly growing and vanished with a frightened squeal.

Ignoring this good advice, Aliyah removed the soggy note from inside the beer bottle and unrolled it. It read:

Stop poking it. You're making it worse.

Warm regards,

Chase & Ronan

Aliyah grabbed a pencil from her bag and scrawled on the back of the note:

Who the fuck are you and what do you want?!!

She shoved the note back into the bottle and pitched it into the Anomaly.

Meanwhile, on the plains of North-West China in the year 1211, on a brisk Thursday morning, the immense forces of the Jin Dynasty were dressed in full battle regalia and lined up along one side of the vast field. The walls of Wusha Fortress towered behind them. Under the command of General Duji Sizhong, they were only forty thousand strong, with the rest of their forces spread out in defensive positions across the length of the Great Wall. Another 400,000 were encamped beyond the ridge in reserve. Some of the men were trained soldiers, but most were conscripted farmers and traders, hunters and fishermen, who had never been in a battle before; but they had come to defend their home, the realm, and the honour of Emperor Xingsheng.

Approaching them on horseback across the field was the Mongol horde of Chinggis (Genghis) Khan. This was a highly trained army of men and women, 100,000 strong, led by the greatest general of the age, who had already, in just five years, proven himself a most formidable adversary. The decisive Battle of Yehuling, otherwise known as the battle of Wild Fox Ridge, was about to begin.

The Khan, riding a magnificent white stallion at the head of his army, raised a hand and the entire horde halted as one behind him with breathtaking military precision. Directly in front of him the Khan noticed a strange anomaly – six-meters wide and swirling with colourful energy. A ball of liquid time. He coaxed his horse slowly forward to get a closer look – *was this some kind of Chinese trick?* As he approached a bottle came flying out of the ball, aimed directly at his head. With lightning reflexes, he caught the bottle before it hit him in the face. If this *was* some Chinese trick it was a very perplexing one – throwing bottles out of invisible floating waters. Khan looked inside the bottle and saw the note. He extracted and opened the roll of paper.

Who the fuck are you and what do you want?!!

Gibberish! Khan crushes the note in his fist and tossed it, enraged. He stuffed the bottle (it was a nice bottle) into his shirt, drew his sabre, and with a terrifying bellow, called the attack: '***KHALDLAGA!!!!!!***'

The Mongols echoed the battle cry as a chilling chorus and charged.

Across the field the Chinese forces responded: '***GONGJI!!!!!***' and charged.

Khan, along with several dozen of his most loyal troops, charged directly at the anomaly. They slashed at it with their swords thinking they could cut it away and power on past it, but instead, they were sucked into its swirling *waters* and vanished from the field.

Meanwhile, back in 2100, the Anomaly started growing again. Ronan and Chase scrambled for the front door of the flat as the expanding sphere burst out of the bedroom and into the living room, consuming the hazard tape and warning sign, taking out side-tables and the couch and anything else in its path, and on through the exterior wall. It had completely overtaken the flat, the rooms around it, the roof above and the floor below, and was on its way to consuming the entire building.

Ronan and Chase ran downstairs as the insatiable ball devoured the third floor, consuming sandstone, metal and wood along the way, and bulged out from the historic edifice over the inner courtyard of Caius College.

Finally, the Anomaly stabilized and settled at a new diameter of fifty metres or so.

'Well, that didn't work,' Ronan said, once they were outside looking up at the corner of the building that had once been their home.

Meanwhile, in New York city in the year 2018, Aliyah emerged from the thirty-second-floor elevator of One NY Plaza, pissed and frazzled. Above the reception desk was the sign *IGT Insurance* in large corporate-blue serifed lettering. It was a very classy firm, and somewhere Aliyah had absolutely no business being. Life insurance was for rich people.

'Excuse me,' the receptionist called as Aliyah marched past with barely a nod, heading straight for the offices within. 'Hello..?!' But she knew it was pointless trying to stop her. This was not the first time Aliyah had made an impromptu visit, and the receptionist knew where she was going.

Beth's office had a magnificent view over the Hudson; you could even see the Statue of Liberty in the harbour. But Aliyah didn't come to look at the view. She burst in to find Beth at her desk staring at some spreadsheets, or whatever it was an actuary spent their day staring at. Aliyah flomped into the comfy chair opposite.

'Aliyah? Something wrong?' While infrequent, Beth had become accustomed to Aliyah sometimes bursting into her office, usually to convey good news, which absolutely had to be done in person. This time seemed different.

'The show's been cancelled!'

'That's a shame.' Beth tried to sound disappointed. 'Why?'

'There's a giant alien... 'bubble' eating the theatre.'

Beth blinked. 'What?'

Aliyah repeated slowly: 'There's a giant alien bubble eating the theatre. And it's getting bigger.'

Beth tried to catch up, but she was still in actuarial mode. 'Well... I suppose that might qualify as an Act of God. But I'd need to know the exact nature of the bubble and where it came from.'

'I'm not here to get your professional advice!'

'Then why are you here?' Beth quickly searched online for any news of an alien 'bubble'.

'Don't you understand? It's growing. It'll eat all of Manhattan pretty soon if they don't stop it.'

'Who?'

'The police. The army. Captain America! Whoever's responsible for this kind of thing.'

'Why was it eating your theatre?'

'Maybe it hates musicals! I don't know!'

Beth found a video – a smartphone recording of Aliyah picking up a beer bottle, writing a note, and throwing the bottle into a giant pulsating … *alien bubble*. 'Holy shit. Is this it?'

'Yeah. Hey, that's me! Fucking huge, isn't it? An hour ago, it was like this big.' Aliyah held up an invisible golf-ball with her fingers.

Beth was still watching the video. 'What are you doing?'

'They threw a beer bottle out, so I threw it back in.'

'Who did?'

'The aliens on the other side,' Aliyah was certain it was aliens.

'A beer bottle?'

'Yeah. With a note.'

'What'd it say?'

'To stop poking it.' Aliyah took a beat. 'There's a thought. How'd they know I poked it?'

'You poked it?'

'Just a little.'

'Why would aliens be throwing beer bottles with notes at you?' Beth asked.

'That's what I wondered. But who can tell with aliens.'

Beth played the video again. 'What did you write back?'

'"Who the fuck are you and what do you want?"'

'That's how you respond to a possible alien invasion?'

'I was pissed.'

'Have you told the police about this?'

'No. Should I?' Then Aliyah saw how many views the video had received. 'Shit, look at the hits. It's nearly a million already!' Then she grimaced. 'Can't see my goddamn face, though. The lighting is terrible.'

'Probably just as well.'

Beth found a live news feed. This showed the scene outside the theatre in Hell's Kitchen, where the bubble had grown to consume half the building and was now eating its way into the street. People could be seen running in a panic from the ever-growing ball of destruction. Beth was horrified. 'My God. From an actuarial perspective this is an unmitigated disaster.'

'Not to mention the actual disaster perspective.'

CHAPTER 5
Welcome, Time Travellers

Meanwhile, in the Fellows' dining room of Gonville & Caius College of Cambridge University, in the year 2009, Sunday June 28th to be specific, at the time of 11:00 am, Professor Stephen Hawking rolled in and surveyed the space. A dull light shone through the high windows. Outside was a typical gloomy English day, but at least it wasn't raining. The room had a high coffered ceiling with an elaborate floral design, supported by fake Greek columns spaced along the walls. Small friezes were nestled between the windows depicting classic poses of semi-clad warriors, damsels and peasants engaged in battle or some other worthy action. The room had the anachronistic air of academic pretence and modern functionalism, which appealed to Professor Hawking's sense of the occasion.

There was a long table down the centre of the room, with chairs to seat up to forty-four guests, and a grandfather clock at one end that reliably chimed the hour. With a flick of his right cheek Professor Hawking's voicebox declared: 'Let's party.'

An army of staff appeared and with great flourish they began to lay out crisp white tablecloths upon which were placed trays of canapes and napkins folded into little peak hats. Several ornate buckets of champaign were brought out, along with clutches of helium-filled balloons – white, purple and blue – tied to weights. These were placed strategically around the room to add a less formal atmosphere to the occasion. A banner was hung over the entrance that read: *Welcome Time Travellers.*

The Time Travellers' Reception, hosted by Professor Hawking at midday on this very day of Sunday June 28th, was about to begin.

Meanwhile, in the year 2100, in the very same dining room, Professor Alice Beauchamp sat at the head of the table, surrounded by several other Professors and administrators of Cambridge University. At the far end of the table stood Chase and Ronan, looking like chastised schoolboys – which indeed they were. There were no balloons or champaign on offer this time, and the weather outside was decidedly stormy, casting a grey pall over the scene. The friezes of Greek heroes looked down on the lads reproachfully, as did the grey-haired and tweed-jacketed academics at the other end of the table.

'Why are we in the dining room, Beauchamp?' asked the Chancellor gruffly, who had arrived late and just sat down.

'All the conference rooms were booked, and this needs to be nutted out now,' Alice Beauchamp said simply, then continued the conversation where they had left off, leaving the Chancellor to catch up. 'Any ideas ladies and gentlemen. Anything at all.'

'Have you tried freezing it?' one of the Professors asked the lads.

Ronan replied. 'Yeah. Blasted it with liquid nitrogen. No go.'

Chase added. 'Heat. Cold. Radio waves. Microwaves. Lasers. It just feeds off them and gets bigger.'

'Can we encase it in glass?' another asked.

Stupid question. 'I think it's a bit late for that,' Chase said diplomatically. 'Plus, I doubt it would work.'

'Don't be so impertinent! We're just trying to help.'

Alice interceded. 'I can see only one solution.' Everyone listened attentively. 'It's a time portal, yes?'

The lads nodded ambivalently – they weren't really sure.

'That was the intention, wasn't it? To build a time portal?'

The lads nodded less ambivalently.

'Into the past.'

'Specifically, June 28th, 2009,' Chase told them.

Alice Beauchamp paused, where had she heard that date? 'Why then?'

Ronan replied, 'That's when the party is.'

'Party?'

'Stephen Hawking's Time Travellers' Reception.'

'Oh... Of course.' Everyone knew about *that* party. Indeed, this was the very room where it happened. Professor Beauchamp smiled, just a little. 'Well then, assuming the Anomaly is a portal between our time and 2009, you need to travel back and change history just enough that your creation of this thing never happens.'

Ronan was confused. 'You want us to go back and…change history?'

'Just your history. If you can.'

'Isn't that a bit drastic?' Chase suggested.

'At the current rate of expansion we estimate the Anomaly will engulf the Earth within – ,' she turned to Doctor Kapoor sitting beside her.

'Five days, two hours and…' Kapoor checked his watch '… fifteen minutes.'

'So yes,' Beauchamp continued. 'Drastic measures are called for.'

44

'I'm not walking into that thing,' Ronan said. 'It's suicide.'

'Why build a portal if you're not going to use it?' Beauchamp reasoned.

'It blew up Felix!'

'Who's Felix?' the Chancellor asked, suddenly panicked. 'Was he a student? Are we insured for that?'

'He was a rat,' Ronan said bluntly. 'A very brave rat. And he didn't deserve to die.' Ronan shot up his hand. 'I vote for more research before sending two potential young Nobel Laureates to what may almost certainly be their untimely death.'

'The only thing that's certain here,' Beauchamp responded coldly, 'is that in a matter of days this thing is going to eat *everything*. You said it yourself, perhaps the entire universe. They don't give prizes for cosmic annihilation.'

Chase, who had remained silent through this, was resigned to their fate. It was their responsibility. He gently touched Ronan's raised arm and coaxed it down. 'How do we do it then?' he said. 'How do we stop ourselves?'

'You're not agreeing to this, are you?' Ronan did not like taking responsibility for things. Even when he should.

'You know the grandfather paradox,' Beauchamp asked.

'You want us to kill our own grandfathers?'

'Or something equally effective. Just make sure neither of you were ever born.'

Ronan was horrified. 'That's murder!'

But Chase saw the logic of it. 'She's right. The only way to stop this is to ensure it never happens in the first place.'

Ronan was not convinced. 'We have no idea what's on the other side of that thing! This is a bad idea.'

Chase remained stoically calm. 'But it's the best bad idea we've got.'

'But...' Ronan was grasping at straws, 'the fact that we *did* invent a time machine means we *don't* succeed in stopping ourselves from inventing a time machine!'

'That's because we haven't done it yet' Chase reasoned. 'But when we do, we'll succeed in stopping ourselves from ever inventing it.'

'– Thus preventing us from being able to travel back in time to stop ourselves!'

'But by then it'll be too late. We'll have already done it.'

'Not if we're never born in the first place!'

'But we are born,' Chase told him reasonably. 'Therefore, we still need to go back and prevent ourselves from ever being born. Once we do, none of this will have ever happened. *We* will have never have happened.'

Ronan couldn't keep up. There was no reckoning out a paradox. '... I guess that makes sense,' he said eventually. 'But how will we know if it's worked?'

'If the Anomaly vanishes,' Beauchamp told them, 'then it's worked.'

Chase agreed. 'Exactly. As long as the Anomaly exists, and keeps growing, we'll know the future hasn't changed. The Time Machine still gets invented.'

'What if we explode – like Felix did?'

'Then the entire planet follows us into oblivion five days later –'

'Five days, two hours and thirteen minutes,' Kapoor clarified.

'– With all of existence close behind,' Chase finished.

Ronan succumbed to the logic. '...Well, when you put it like that.'

Five minutes later, Chase and Ronan stood before the Anomaly, a giant swirling sphere of cosmic destruction that, since they last saw it, had consumed half the building. The Professors, Administrators and Chancellor stood by anxiously.

Beauchamp approached. 'No time to waste,' she told the lads.

Ronan laughed. 'Ha! I get it now.'

Alice didn't. 'We're counting on you,' she told them both. 'The whole world is counting on you. So don't fuck it up!'

'We'll do our best,' Ronan said.

'And don't take this the wrong way,' Beauchamp said, 'but I hope I never see you again.'

Chase understood, nodded. 'Come on, Ronan.'

The lads stepped forward and confronted the Anomaly, now just a few feet away. It swirled ominously.

Ronan turned to his friend. 'Chase?'

'Yeah?'

'I'm scared.'

'Me too.'

'If we don't survive this, I want you to know –'

– then Professor Beauchamp pushed them both in.

CHAPTER 6
New York Fuckin' City

Chase and Ronan tumbled into the portal screaming and clinging desperately to one another. They were not falling exactly – gravity didn't exist within the vortex – but the momentum of Professor Beauchamp's push gave them a sense of plummeting freefall. Once they stopped screaming, the lads realised they weren't dead and looked about. They found themselves inside a huge 'space' that was somehow bigger on the inside than the exterior of the Anomaly suggested. They could make out other figures swirling around the vortex – people, horses, *Genghis Khan?* But before they could get too accustomed, they were ejected from the vortex –

– and spilled out the pavement of 12th Avenue in New York City in the year 2018, outside what had once been a gay night club in Hell's Kitchen, now re-dubbed The Pagan Playhouse. The theatre itself was gone. Indeed, most of the block was now gone, consumed by the growing bubble.

The lads tried to see where they had landed but were blinded by an intense light. Squinting, they found themselves surrounded by barricades, floodlights, police in riot gear, soldiers with automatic weapons, jeeps with mounted machine guns, tanks with cannons, even an aircraft carrier in the nearby waters, all with their weapons aimed directly at them; everything a panicked America would deploy for a suspected alien invasion. Behind the barricades and wall of military intervention was a seething mass of curious onlookers, there to witness the end of the world, and record it for posterity on their smartphones.

Chase and Ronan slowly raised their hands as they got to their feet, confused and just a little terrified.

'What were you gonna say?' Chase asked.

'Huh?'

'You said: 'If we don't survive this, you want me to know ...' what? What do you want me to know?'

'I'll tell you later,' Ronan said as he stared down the barrel of a tank five meters from his face.

A figure stepped forward to confront them. This was General Wainwright of the US army, though to the lads he was just a silhouetted blur who seemed to be wearing some kind of uniform. He said, very loudly: '**DERYACMNPAAYYSS?**'

The lads covered their ears against the assault of distorted sound. '... What?!'

'**DERYACMNPAAYYSS?**'

Chase and Ronan looked at each other, baffled. 'Can you understand what he's saying?' Chased asked Ronan.

'Not a word.'

'Perhaps it's a foreign language.'

Chase called out: 'Do you speak English?!'

General Wainwright lowered his megaphone and asked again: 'Do you come in peace?!'

'Oh, yeah... Sure... of course.'

The General spoke very slowly. 'Who are you and where are you from?!'

'He sounds American,' Ronan mused. 'Why does he sound American?'

Chase shouted back: 'Well, I'm Chase. And he's Ronan! –'

'Hi,' Ronan waved.

'– And we're from Cambridge!'

'The one in England!' Ronan added.

'And, if you don't mind my asking,' Chase continued, 'where are we, exactly?!'

The General answered proudly, 'This is New York City! In the United States of America! Planet Earth!' Then added, 'Welcome!'

'Right planet, wrong country,' Ronan murmured.

'Thank you,' Chase called to the man. 'And…*when* are we?!'

'Yeah, what year is this?!'

'It is the year two-thousand and eighteen!' the General answered.

Chase turned to Ronan. 'How the fuck did we end up here?'

'Dunno.'

'We're out by nine years and three thousand miles.'

'Still, we did it.'

'You're right,' Chase grinned. 'We just travelled through time.'

'Take that, Space-Time Continuum!'

The lads high-fived. Suddenly all the weapons trained on them cocked and loaded, ready to fire. The lads raised their arms as high as they could, signalling their acquiescent surrender.

Moments later Chase and Ronan found themselves handcuffed in the back of a New York City paddy wagon, with two police officers sitting opposite, eyeing them warily.

'Where are your grandparents?' Chased asked Ronan.

'I don't think they're born yet.'

'But where's your family?'

'Belfast.'

'Mine's in Liverpool... I think.'

'You think?'

'I don't really know much about them,' Chase admitted.

'Still,' Ronan conceded. 'Liverpool. How are we gonna get back to England in less than five days, find our ancestors, whoever and wherever they are, kill them – ' the police officers reacted, '– and get back to our own time?'

Chase addressed the officers. 'Don't worry. It's just a game we're playing.'

'Oh yeah,' Ronan elaborated. 'It's called Fuck the Future. You play the part of a time traveller who has to mess up history so bad that you were never born in the first place. First one to die wins.'

Chase had an idea. 'Precisely.'

'Huh?'

'We don't have to kill our grandparents, provided we can change things enough that they never meet, or have kids, or any number of other butterfly effects that prevent us from being born or creating the machine.'

Ronan raised his handcuffed wrists. 'And how are we gonna do that?'

Meanwhile, across town, Aliyah and Beth exited the elevator of their apartment building and tramped down the creamy carpeted corridor, both of them head down as they scrolled through news feeds on their phones.

'Okay, so they're not aliens,' Beth confirmed. 'They're from England apparently.'

'I think they're time travellers,' Aliyah said.

'They're not time travellers.'

'They had to ask what year it was.'

'Maybe they've been locked in a mental institute for the past ten years.'

'Then how do you explain the note?' Aliyah challenged.

'That doesn't prove they're time travellers. Just that they drink beer and write stupid notes. I think that show you're working on has gone to your head.'

'If they came out of that bubble thing, then they must know what it is and how to stop it.'

'Or maybe they just fell into it and have no idea what it is.' Beth really didn't want to get involved. 'I say let the army handle it. They're the experts.'

'Remember what the note said,' Aliyah insisted. 'To stop poking it. What do you think the army are gonna do?'

They opened the door to their apartment and discovered three men-in-black (one of whom was a woman) waiting for them in their living room. The woman stepped forward. 'Aliyah Alexander?'

The girls froze.

Meanwhile, on the deck of the Titanic in the year 1912, specifically the 15th of April, 1:18am, one hour and thirty-eight minutes after hitting the iceberg, panicked passengers fought over the few remaining lifeboats. Most of the boats, only half-laden with women and children, had been cast off already and could be seen drifting away from the ship. With just a few boats remaining, some of the more cowardly men could be seen fighting for a place or jumping the rail into the icy waters out of desperation. Off the starboard side of the ship, near where the iceberg had ripped into the hull, another instance of the Anomaly could be seen consuming the crippled vessel. Nearby, the band played the cheerful *Glow-Worm* by Paul Lincke to accompany the disaster, while the Anomaly grew and swirled in response to the music like a dancing orb.

Wandering the deck of the sinking vessel was a very confused, and rather green-looking census-taker from the Middle Ages – Edmund Constable. After being plucked from his time by the Anomaly, he somehow found himself aboard the doomed vessel in the early 20th century. Edmund staggered about on the heaving ship, then finally leaned into the railing, and threw up over the side. He grabbed a passing man dressed in a strange, though excellently tailored, black suit. 'Where am I?!' he demanded. 'What's happening?!'

'The ship's sinking you fool! We're all gonna die!' The man ran off, the tails of his coat flapping after him.

Edmund looked about in astonishment. 'This is a *ship*?!'

He wandered up the listing deck in a daze, oblivious to the chaos around him, until he came upon a crowd of people clamouring over one of the last remaining lifeboats. Among them was a well-dressed first-class passenger known to history as 'Molly' (Maggie to her friends) Brown. She was helping others into the boat when she spotted Edmund. 'Come on. There's still room.'

Edmund approached. 'Brave madam, pray tell. Am I dead? Are you an Angel?'

Maggie smiled at him. 'I'm no angel, sweetie. But thanks for the compliment. Come on. You might as well jump in with us.' She reached out to him, but just then the ship lurched, and Edmund was thrown down the steeply listing deck towards the Anomaly. Several other people also lost their footing and slid into the bubble – including the band, who continued playing fearlessly as their chairs slid into the abyss of swirling spacetime.

Edmund, unable to find purchase on the slippery deck, tumbled in after them –

– Edmund sank and soared like a rag doll swept up by the apocalypse. He found himself surrounded by light and colour, an unearthly discord of sound, and the ominous sense that he was about to be ejected into Paradise or cast into Hell. Those who fell in with him all flew off in different directions, some screaming in terror, others silent with awe. The musicians abandoned their song and clung to their instruments as they tumbled off into the swirling abyss. Edmund glimpsed people and creatures from other times and places; a harvesting of ensnared souls from antiquity and far-flung lands, all trapped in the supernatural whirlwind.

Edmund was ejected from the whirlwind onto –

– A backstreet of Hell's Kitchen, New York City, in the year 2018. It was night, and Edmund found himself surrounded by strange colourful four-wheeled carts, all parked in rows, with not a single horse in sight.

He looked about but saw no-one. At least the ground wasn't shifting under his feet anymore. It didn't look like Paradise, but he had expected Hell to be more…hellish.

Edmund stepped away from the Doomsday Bubble, which had grown to the size of a small building and was now eating into what the locals (he would later discover) called a carpark situated at the rear of a Pagan Playhouse. Touching one of the vehicles, he marvelled at how smooth and cold it was. Glass windows revealed a luxurious interior, and the glass itself was astonishingly flat and even; he'd never seen such masterful workmanship. Even the wheels were of a strange design and make. There appeared to be no wood at all on the vehicle, as if it were made entirely of copper or bronze. But it was so large. And there were so many of them. Truly this was not the same land he had come from.

'Where'd *you* come from?'

Edmund ducked behind one of the vehicles. 'Who said that?'

Out of the shadows a strange, disconcerting rattle started. A man with long unkempt hair and beard and dressed in colourful rags stepped out, pushing before him a small cart that was the source of the rattle. It was filled with all manner of things – clothing and blankets, and strange packages with pictures of what appeared to be foodstuffs on them, and boxes and bags piled high or hanging over the sides. The man looked like one of the peasants of York Edmund had recently been interviewing, though dirtier and wealthier, judging by his possessions.

Edmund rose and anxiously stepped into the light to greet the man. He smiled warmly and bowed, 'Good evening, sir. My name is Edmund Constable.'

The man said nothing.

'And you are?'

The man came closer, his cart rattling unnervingly, then stopped. Edmund could smell him from three meters away.

'You come outta that thing?' the man asked.

The accent was strange. Edmund had a hard time understanding him. 'Why yes actually. You wouldn't happen to know what it is?'

'Big fuckin' ball.'

'Yes. The ball. Do you know where it came from?'

'Aliens they reckon.'

Edmund didn't understand so tried another tack. 'Can you tell me what town this is?'

'Huh?'

'By what name is this town called?'

'Town? This is New York fuckin' city, man.'

Edmund could only make out one word in the man's ramble. 'York. Did you say York? Ah! Now I can get my bearings. Though, I was recently in York, and I must confess this looks rather different to how I remember it.'

'You talk funny.'

'Can you direct me to the Castle of King William?' Edmund knew a castle had just recently been completed in the city.

'And you dress funny. You goin' to a costume party?'

'I beg your pardon?'

'What's with the getup? You an actor or somethin'?'

Judging by his florid gesture Edmund guessed the man was referring to his clothes. 'This is my usual attire. Has the fashion in York changed so much that you find it passé?'

'Passé? It's positively archaic. So what's in there?' the man nodded.

'I don't follow you.'

The man pointed at the Anomaly. 'In that thing? You came out of it, didn't you?'

'Ah... Yes.'

'So what's in there?'

'I cannot fathom if this is the work of God or the Devil. But it is beyond my meagre understanding.'

'You always talk like that? Or are you like, you know, *Method*.'

York certainly has changed, Edmund thought. 'Can you tell me, please, where I might find the Lord of these parts?'

'We ain't got no Lords.'

'Who is your liege?... Your ruler?'

'Oh. Him. Up that way, about eight blocks. Can't miss it.'

'Thank you, good sir. You have been most helpful.'

Edmund headed as directed and did not hear the homeless man's last words; not that he would have understood them anyway.

'...Bloody tourist.'

Edmund walked eastward up West 51st. The buildings were astonishingly tall, creating great canyons with a hard black pitch or smooth stone covering the ground, and strange signs and lamps marking each corner. It seemed every avenue he crossed had no name, just a number, and it was all very ... *square*. A uniform lattice of wide thoroughfares. Very practical, Edmund thought, though rather unimaginative. This was definitely not the York he remembered.

The place was strangely beautiful and ugly at the same time, with prosperous trees lining the street on both sides, or bizarre art and dilapidated frontages breaking up the endless high walls of the towering structures. As overwhelming and alien as the streets and buildings were, the thing that most troubled Edmund was that he was so alone. The place was devoid of any other living creature. He could see lights high up in some of the buildings and heard strange distant noises he could not place, but, aside from the one man he had spoken to when first arriving, there was not another soul about. The city was deserted.

Eventually, at the corner of the road marked as the 52nd, he came upon an oddly familiar sight – a grand cathedral in the modern gothic style. He paused in the middle of the street to look up at the magnificent edifice. It was quite out of place in this city of glass and stone and pitch, and Edmund thanked the Lord for it. He abandoned his quest for the leader of the city and decided to find refuge in the house of God. Surely a priest would be more understanding of his dilemma than the local lord.

Just then one of the strange carts came speeding at him, bleating and honking terribly as if to herald its approach. Edmund jumped out of the way just in time, and watched it tear past at astonishing speed, especially considering there was not a single horse at the head. As he watched it speed off, Edmund heard a rumbling approach from behind him. Turning he saw another unexpected sight – a massive herd of bison stampeding up 52nd.

Edmund ran.

The bison crashed and pummelled parked vehicles in their path, leaving a cacophony of chaos and shattered glass in their wake.

Edmund ran faster… but not fast enough.

The herd thundered up behind and overtook him. Edmund found himself running with the beasts, surrounded by terrified stampeding bison who's pumping shoulders reached over his head. He feared he would be trampled at any moment, but the bison treated him as if he were one of them, avoiding the human in their midst and running past until they eventually pulled ahead, and Edmund was mercifully alone once more watching the stampede recede. He slowed and caught his breath. *That was close.*

Then he heard, and saw, what they were running from. Edmund had no words to describe what later generations would call a Tyrannosaurus Rex. To him it was just a monster with the biggest teeth he had ever seen, and a roar so terrifying it caused Edmund to soil himself. It was a dragon on two legs, with an enormous head and strangely puny arms. The misshapen dragon looked down at him as he stood alone and helpless in the middle of the street. It opened its jaws ready to snap him up.

Edmund screamed like a woman and ran into the nearest glass tower. It had a luminous gold-plated entrance set back from the street, with strange revolving doors he had to push through.

The dragon gave chase. It knocked down a small clock tower that stood out the front, tripped, and smashed its bulbous head into the upper part of the entrance, knocking loose some of the lettering that adorned it. A giant gold 'T' fell to the ground, leaving behind a golden simile of the posterior.

Edmund ran deep into the lobby of the tower, skidding to a stop on the polished marble floor, thinking he was safe – the glass and stone would protect him. But the dragon didn't stop. It followed him into the building, leaping over the doors and smashing through the tall glass above, causing a shower of tiny shards as the window exploded into a million pieces. The dragon stumbled as its giant head became ensnared by a tapestry of stars and stripes hanging above the entrance. Blinded, the dragon fell in a heap, ripping the tapestry from its fitting and crashing to the floor right in front of Edmund.

Edmund screamed like a woman again. And soiled himself… again.

Fearing he would be trapped in here with the beast he took advantage of its temporary blindness, running around it and back out through the slowly revolving doors. The dragon recovered, getting to its feet; but the tapestry was still wrapped around its head, and its tiny arms could not reach to pull it away. It thrashed about wildly, colliding with gold and marble walls, leaving huge dents and cracks wherever it struck. It stumbled into the building, destroying everything in its wake and sounding the way you might expect an angry, blinded dragon to sound, eventually colliding with a rather infamous escalator and ripping it to pieces.

But Edmund didn't stick around to watch. He followed the bison down the street, away from the scene, only to be stopped by a sudden blaze of light and the sound of a new monster that growled with the clamour of a hundred voices – a convoy of battle wagons blocking his path. Edmund froze. *Now what!?*

The lead vehicle bleated at him the way that earlier cart had, though this time it was deeper and more intimidating.

'CLRRRTHWAAAYSSZZNN ... CLRRTHWAAAYYY!'

More bleating.

General Wainwright stepped out of the vehicle, lowered his megaphone and shouted. 'Clear the way, you idiot!'

'Is someone there?' Edmund couldn't see a thing.

The General stepped into the light. Edmund could just make out a human silhouette wearing some kind of uniform.

'Get out of the way!'

'Forgive me, my lord. I must confess the power of your lamp quite startled me. And your unusual wagon is something I – ' Edmund was interrupted as several soldiers emerged from the light and surrounded him; their odd, blunt weapons pointed at him.

The General stepped close enough that Edmund could now make out his face. He looked Edmund up and down. Edmund could tell from his bearing he was a man of some authority, but he was not the Lord of the city – more a military underling. Edmund judged it best to avoid saying anything more until he had a better idea of exactly where he was.

'Where are you from?' The General asked.

'I wish to speak with your lord. I think it best I say nothing more –' again he was interrupted and soon found himself thrown into the back of one of the horseless wagons, with metal bands about his wrists, and two equally bemused young men as company.

Chase and Ronan lifted their fellow prisoner off the floor of the paddy wagon and helped him to the bench. The two officers sat opposite, silently watching.

'Hello,' Ronan greeted cheerfully.

'Good day to you, sir.'

Ronan sniffed. 'Is that you?'

Edmund dropped his head in shame. 'There was a dragon. I lost control of myself.'

'A dragon?'

'I don't know what else to call it. It was quite terrifying.'

'That's okay,' Ronan reassured. 'I probably would have shit myself too if I saw a real dragon.'

Edmund was both shocked and heartened at the stranger's uncouth empathy. 'My name is Edmund Constable.'

"I'm Ronan. He's Chase.'

'Hi there,' said Chase, raising his manacled wrists. 'Welcome to the end-times.'

Finally, Edmund thought, *civilised people*. Their dialects were strange again, but somehow more comprehensible. 'Can you tell me, please, will this carriage convey us to the Lord of this city where I can plead my case? I confess to being at something of a loss as to where I am and how I got here.'

'I doubt it.'

'Besides, we can tell you all that.'

'Were you also delivered here by the Doomsday Bubble?' This turn of phrase piqued Chase and Ronan's interest. 'I call it that for want of a better name, as I cannot fathom its true nature.'

'Actually,' Ronan conceded, 'that pretty much sums it up.'

'You know whereof I speak?'

'Yeah. We built it,' Chase confessed.

Edmund's cheerful demeanour vanished as he glared at Chase. '...Why?'

CHAPTER 7
Take the Day

Meanwhile, in the Fellows' dining room of Gonville & Caius College of Cambridge University, in the year 2009, Sunday June 28th, at 11:30 am according to the grandfather clock, Professor Stephen Hawking looked about the now fully decorated and prepped room for his Time Travellers' reception.

'Will there be anything else, Professor Hawking?' asked the head waiter.

The professor twitched his right cheek and a few seconds later the voicebox declared, 'That is all for now. Thank you.'

The head waiter bowed slightly, leaving Professor Hawking alone in the room, where he waited for his guests to arrive.

Meanwhile, in the year 2018, in a secret facility somewhere outside of New York City, Chase, Ronan and Edmund found themselves detained in a stark, puritanical, white room, like something out of a Stanley Kubrick nightmare. Everything was white. The table and chairs were white. The walls, floor and ceiling were white. The surveillance cameras in the corners of the ceiling were white. Even the two-way mirror overlooking the room was somehow white. The room was so white it hurt the eyes, and so quiet even the noise was white. The only non-white things in the room were Chase, Ronan and Edmund, who sat around the table looking forlornly at each other because there was nothing else to focus on.

They remained silent for the longest time.

Finally, Edmund said softly: 'The privy here is quite remarkable.' Despite their stony silence, the soldiers had allowed them a bathroom break, supplying Edmund with some clean underwear. 'And the undergarments they gave me are very…snug.'

'That's the future for you – indoor plumbing and elastic.'

The future. 'I do not think they believed your story,' Edmund said. 'In fact, I do not think *I* believe your story.'

'I wouldn't.' Ronan murmured. Chase grumbled. 'Face it, Chase. We sound like lunatics. No one's ever gonna believe we're time travellers from the future.'

The white door opened, and Aliyah Alexander was shoved into the room. The door closed and locked behind her. She appeared confused and pissed. Squinting, she scanned the room. 'Jesus, this is whiter than a Klan meeting.' She fixed her gaze on the men at the table, if only because there was nothing else to fix one's gaze upon. She recognised two of them from the news and clicked her tongue. 'Figures.'

Edmund spoke first. 'Did you come from the Doomsday Bubble as well?'

'The what?'

'That's what we're calling the Anomaly,' Ronan explained. 'Has a nice ring to it, don't you think?'

Aliyah joined them at the table, struggling to see the white chair against the white table and white floor. 'No. I didn't come from the Doomsday Bubble. I just poked it.'

Ronan threw up his hands. 'That's half the problem, right there! Everyone keeps poking the damn thing.'

'Are you the ones who sent the message?'

'The message in a bottle? You got it?'

'Yeah. Did you get my reply?'

'... No. What did you say?'

Aliyah sighed. 'Doesn't matter now. So what is this Doomsday Bubble exactly?'

'It's a time portal,' Ronan explained. 'We're from the future, Chase and me. I'm Ronan, by the way. Edmund here comes from the Middle Ages.'

'In the year of our Lord, ten-eighty-six,' Edmund bowed his head.

Aliyah could run with that, it sounded bizarre enough to be true. 'So there's more of these portals out there? In different times?'

'Several it seems.' Ronan was impressed. 'I must say you have a very fine grasp of the situation. Are you a physicist by any chance?'

'Actress. Triple threat. Name's Aliyah.' They shook hands. She nodded towards Chase. 'What's with him? Doesn't he talk?'

'He's thinking. He goes quiet when he's thinking.'

'What's he thinking about?'

'How we're going to save the world in less than five days.'

'Five days?'

'That's when the Anomaly – the Doomsday Bubble – will engulf the entire planet.'

Aliyah froze for a second. '... You're shitting me.'

Edmund winced. Even the women here were uncouth.

''Fraid not.'

'Why would you create something that's going to destroy the planet?'

'The whole universe, actually.'

Aliyah was aghast.

'That was my reaction,' Edmund said.

'Well, it's not like we meant it,' Ronan's voice went up an octave.

'So how are you going to fix it?' Aliyah demanded.

'We do have a plan. But it's a bit hard to do stuck in here.'

'Let me guess. You came back in time to change the past so that you never create the Doomsday Bubble in the first place.'

'You're very good at this.'

'I've seen *Back to the Future*. So Chase, any idea how to get us out of here?'

Chase turned to Aliyah. 'Yes, actually.' He pulled from his sleeve a device that looked something like an electric screwdriver.

Ronan didn't recognise it. 'What's that?'

'I call it a Pod – a Programmable Omni-Functional Device. P.O.D. Pod.'

'That sounds promising,' Ronan gleamed.

'It's just a prototype. I still haven't worked out all the kinks.'

'So, it's like a sonic screwdriver,' Aliyah posited, using a cultural reference none of them got.

Chase suppressed a laugh, then said diplomatically. 'Nothing so crude as that.'

'Can it get us out of here?' Ronan asked.

'I think so,' Chase said.

'You sly devil. Why didn't you whip that out earlier?'

'I couldn't get to it before now.'

Ronan was confused. 'Why? Where were you hiding it?'

The door burst open and two burly soldiers rushed them, making directly for Chase. They must have been listening. Chase raised the Pod, pressed a button, and the two men collapsed to the floor in unconscious heaps.

Edmund was horrified.

Aliyah was agog. 'Brilliant!'

'Don't worry. They'll recover. Let's go!'

Moments later, an alarm sounded outside the secret facility while searchlights desperately scanned the grounds. Chase, Ronan, Aliyah and Edmund ran from a freshly carved hole in the wall towards the chain-link fence that surrounded the compound.

'That was just brilliant!'' Aliyah enthused. 'I mean, who knew future tech would be so... fucking brilliant!'

'I think I believe you now,' Edmund admitted.

'Never doubt an Irishman,' Ronan declared.

Chase flipped a setting and pointed the Pod at the fence, causing it to 'magically' unravel, creating a hole they could pass through.

'Brilliant!'

They all squeezed through the fence and escaped.

Meanwhile, back in their over-priced New York apartment, Beth was woken by her phone. She grumbled, saw who it was and answered. 'Aliyah. Are you okay? What happened?'

'Beth. You still got that book on the history of everything?'

'Huh?'

'You know, the one with all the stats.'

'You mean: "A statistical analysis of the consequences of major historical events upon culture, society and the environment – second edition"?'

'Yeah, that one. Can you grab it, and meet me at the place with the thing?'

'What place?'

'You know. Where we went that time.'

'Which time?'

'The time we went where the thing was. The place with the thing.'

Beth was lost, and still half asleep. 'Can't you just tell me?'

'They might be listening.'

'Who might be listening?'

'You know – them.'

'Why would they be listening?'

'Because that's what they do.'

Beth couldn't fault Aliyah's logic. 'Okay. So, the place with the thing where we went that time.'

'That's it. And bring the book. See you soon.' Aliyah hung up.

Beth still didn't know where she meant ... then it came to her. '... Ahhh.'

Half an hour later – give or take – Beth arrived, hastily dressed and made up, at the place: *The Bitter End* nightclub in Greenwich Village. It was a somewhat legendary spot, famed for its exposed red-brick wall at the back of the stage, and featuring a range of jazz, blues or rock bands who always played too loud for conversation. But then, that was the point. Tonight, the bill included a funky blues-rock ensemble complete with keyboards, brass section, backup singers, and a black lead singer who prowled the low, wide proscenium stage wearing an outrageous single-piece jumpsuit that harkened back to the best and worst of 70's funk. Despite all that (or perhaps because of it) they were pretty good, and seemed to be unaffected by the fact that the club was practically deserted.

The 'thing' Aliyah was referring to was a skeleton. The night they went there some five months prior there had been a skeleton on stage. Not performing, obviously, but sitting comfortably at the back of the stage as if observing the show. It didn't move, and no-one in the band drew attention to it. It was just there. Aliyah found it fascinating. She called it Mister Bones, and thought he was the best part of the entire show – upstaging everyone by not doing a damn thing. She'd said it was a great lesson for her as an actress – the less you do the more compelling you become.

So that was the place with the thing. Getting there was not difficult, the subway was still running, though it was strangely empty. The news feed Beth watched on her journey down to the Village showed her that more had apparently emerged from Aliyah's alien bubble beyond the two English 'time travellers'. Wild animals were roaming the streets and people from different eras of history were apparently wandering about lost and confused. Given New York had largely shut down over the crisis, Beth was surprised to find *The Bitter End* open for business – perhaps it was a sign.

She spotted Aliyah at back of the room sitting with three men – of course. Two of them Beth recognised from the news. 'Aren't these the guys from the giant ball?!' she shouted over the band as she joined them.

'We're calling it a Doomsday Bubble!' Aliyah bellowed cheerfully.

'That sounds ominous!' Beth watched the third man, dressed in something from the Middle Ages, as he poked at a hamburger with a fork while bobbing his head to the music.

Aliyah did the introductions. 'Guys, this is my best friend in the world and nerd extraordinaire – Beth. Beth, this is Ronan, Chase, and Edmund.'

'Hi!' Ronan waved.

'Greetings,' Edmund bowed.

Ronan nudged Chase. 'Hello.' Chase nodded distractedly.

'What are you doing?' Beth asked him, curious. 'And what is that? Some kind of smart…stick?'

'Spot on!' Ronan answered, then to Edmund: 'Eat your burger, it won't kill you.'

Edmund picked up the hamburger with his right hand and took a bite.

'Did he come out of the bubble as well?' Beth asked.

'I am from the year of our lord, ten-eighty-six,' Edmund said through a mouthful. 'Hmm. It's good.'

'Did you bring the book?!' Aliyah asked.

'Yeah!'

Ronan grabbed the volume as Beth pulled it from her bag. 'Great. Thanks!' Ronan immediately started to pour through its pages.

'You also have a domesday book?' Edmund asked.

Beth knew exactly what he was talking about. 'Kind of. Though this one's more a record of people's actions rather than their holdings.'

Edmund nodded understanding and took another bite from his burger. For some reason he was better able to comprehend Beth, despite (or perhaps because of) her Virginia accent.

Chase meanwhile was preoccupied with the Pod which was projecting a holographic keyboard and screen. He was reprogramming it.

The band finished their song. Aliyah stood and applauded loudly, then whistled. Edmund followed her lead. 'Excellent work, minstrels! Very lively!'

Aliyah pulled Edmund back into his seat. 'Don't say that.'

'Say what?'

'Don't call them minstrels.'

Edmund didn't understand.

The singer announced to the near empty room: 'We're gonna take a break now. But we'll be back soon... Maybe.' The band headed straight for the bar.

'We need your help, Beth,' Aliyah said.

'Of course you do. The world's coming to an end and you want to organize a double date.'

'How did you know? About the world coming to an end, I mean. Not the double date. That's not what this is. If it were it'd have to be a triple date, and frankly I don't know who would be a good match for Edmund here. Unless you're gay. If you're gay I know someone who'd be perfect for you.'

Edmund was getting used the local dialect, but still had no idea what she was saying. 'I... try to keep a positive outlook on things.'

'He's a real Monty Python freak,' Aliyah continued, selling Edmund on the idea. 'And he's got that whole steampunk goth thing down. You should meet him.'

'Aliyah, focus,' Beth interrupted. 'What do you mean the world's coming to an end?'

'The Doomsday Bubble. In five days – '

' – four now,' Ronan corrected.

'– that thing's gonna eat the whole planet. So it's up to us to stop it.'

'What about the army? What about those guys in our apartment?'

'All they did was lock us up and waste valuable time.'

Ronan mused enigmatically 'Wasting time...'

'Why would they do that?'

'They're the army. That's what they do. We'd be on our way to Guantanamo if we hadn't escaped.'

'You escaped? How?'

'You wouldn't believe me if I told you. It was brilliant.'

'But time travellers from the future creating a... Doomsday Bubble that'll destroy the planet in five – '

' – four – '

'– days is credible?'

'And Donald Trump is President. Go figure.'

Beth couldn't argue with that. The world was indeed coming to an end. 'Well, that thing's reached 52nd Street and there seems to be no stopping it, so what's the plan?'

'You're the history buff. From a statistical point of view, what single event has had the most profound impact on history?'

For the first time Ronan lifted his nose out of the book and listened attentively.

'There's been lots. How far back do you want to go?'

'Something recent,' Ronan said. 'Something that affected the whole world. But especially the UK.'

'Ahh... World War Two?'

Edmund blanched.

'Of course!' Aliyah declared. 'Kill Hitler!'

'Who's Hitler?' Edmund asked, while the band at the bar looked at them curiously.

'Long story,' Aliyah waved away.

Ronan flipped through the book. 'Where do I find that?'

'Give it here.' Beth took the volume from him and instantly turned to the correct section and relevant entry. 'Statistically the best time to do it, if we're trying to avoid the war completely, would be to stop the Nazi's before they rise to power. So... the Beer Hall Putsch of 1923.'

'The Beer Hall what?'

'It was a failed coup attempt. But it set Hitler on the path.'

'Okay,' Ronan declared. 'The Beer Hall Push it is.'

'Putsch.'

'Whatever.'

'But you can't be serious,' Beth snubbed.

'Done,' Chase said as he swiped away the Holo-Display and held up the Pod.

'Done what, exactly?'

'I've programmed the Pod to be a Temporal Navigator. It should help guide us through the Anomaly to wherever we're going. So where are we going?'

Beth checked the entry again. 'November 8th, 1923. Munich.' She handed the book back to Ronan.

'Uh... You have to come with us,' he told her. 'I can't make head or tail of this thing.'

'But I have work in the morning.'

Aliyah looked at her friend. 'New York is shutting down if you hadn't noticed. I doubt they'll be open.'

'Of course they'll be open. It's insurance. It's times like these people need us the most.'

'Come on, Beth. Take the day,' Aliyah said. 'Let's go kill Hitler.'

Edmund was thoroughly confused. 'Who's Hitler? And what is World War Two?'

CHAPTER 8
Jude!

The Tourneau Time Machine shop on West 57th was the world's largest watch store. It began as a small family business in Russia in 1900 until, after the Bolshevik Revolution, the Tourneau brothers found their way to New York in 1924. In fact, it wasn't even a watch store to begin with, just a corner of a dress-shop in the Berkshire Place Hotel on 52nd and Madison. But the business grew to have thirty-four stores across the country and its own custom line of timepieces. This store on West 57th opened in 1997. The facade was emblazoned with 22 traditional analog clocks showing the time for different cities around the world, along with a giant clock, front and centre, displaying the current New York time. The old-fashioned clock-faces harkened to a bygone era of art-deco and painstaking craftsmanship. But the passage of time is inevitable no matter when or where you are, and change moves through history like a virus. In less than three years this famous façade would be gone – bought out and updated to something more modern and less remarkable. There was no stopping the march of progress. Or at least, that *would* be the case, if it were not for the present crisis, where the building and its clocks were to be consumed in less than three minutes.

Chase, Ronan, Aliyah, Beth and Edmund all stood on the otherwise abandoned street, looking up at the clocks. The time in New York, according to the big clock, was ten minutes past one in the morning. It looked like it was smiling at them. The Doomsday Bubble, now ten-stories high, could be seen encroaching from the south-west. It had eaten through Columbus Circle and the South-West corner of Central Park. Lincoln Centre was gone and to the east Rockefeller Centre. Times Square and Broadway were also lost.

'The damn thing ate Broadway,' Aliyah cried. 'Broadway is gone!'

The bubble swirled and swelled. Its growth had been in fits and starts at first, but now it seemed to just keep on growing as all manner of things fell into and out of it. It had eaten through Tiffany's next door and now started consuming the clocks on the façade of Tourneau's.

A man stumbled out of the Bubble. He was dressed in blue jeans, a white t-shirt under a leather vest with tassels, and had a dark blue fedora set back on his head. A tangle of light-brown hair flowed down his back and over his shoulders. He looked like a hippie from Woodstock '69 having a bad trip, as he spun about bewildered and awed. 'Whoa... man! What just happened?'

The others ignored him.

'This'll change the world for everyone, won't it?' Aliyah said.

'What would you prefer?' Ronan countered. 'A completely different planet, or no planet at all?'

The hippie circled in confusion. 'Hey? What happened to the light show?'

'So we've no choice, really,' Aliyah intoned. 'To fix the future, we have to fuck with the past.'

'Yep.'

'Hey Man! Stay away from the brown acid! It really messes with your perception of reality.'

'We should hold hands,' Edmund suggested. 'So we don't get separated.'

'Good idea.'

They joined hands, with Chase at one end of the line, his free hand holding the Pod.

'Beautiful, man. Let's all join hands.' The hippie spun around and only now realized he was no longer where he once had been. 'Hey? Where'd everyone go? Where's the band?' He approached the others.

'What's it like?' Aliyah was suddenly nervous.

'Like being caught in a riptide,' Ronan told her. 'Don't fight it. Just let it pull you along.'

Chase tapped a few buttons on the Pod. 'Coordinates set. Let's hope this works.'

'I can't believe I'm doing this,' Beth complained. 'I hate travel.'

'I'm glad you're here,' Aliyah squeezed her hand. The girls exchanged a look of solidarity.

The hippie stepped up to Ronan. 'Hey, man? Have the Dead been on yet? And which way's the stage? I got a bit lost.'

'Come on!' Chase, holding the Pod ahead of him, led them into the Doomsday Bubble. They each tightened their grip as they marched (and then were sucked) to an uncertain fate.

The hippie watched them go, noticing the Anomaly for the first time. 'Whoa! That's a big fuckin' bubble.'

He poked it and was promptly sucked in after the others.

Our five intrepid travellers – hands tightly clasped – were tossed and tumbled along the eddies of the time current. Chase was at the head leading the way, arm outstretched, the Pod pulling them along. Around them they could see hundreds of other accidental travellers caught up in the vortex, all swishing about and being dispatched to different spacetime instances of the Anomaly. There were families, armies, peasant and noble. People from Europe, Asia, Africa, the Americas, and from every time and place in between. No part of history it seemed was untouched. There were animals and birds and creatures of the sea, all tumbling about among all the human flotsam – a blue whale here, a Bengal tiger there. Dogs and dinosaurs, dolphins and dodos. As well as trees and houses, airplanes and penguins. The vortex was becoming quite crowded.

The hippie who had fallen in after our travellers spun away from them. 'This is a really bad trip, man!' he cried as he fell out of the vortex to some unknown time and place.

The Pod led our team toward another part of the vortex and ejected them to –

– Odeonsplatz square, Munich, November 9, 1923. 11:15am. A Friday. The travellers tumbled out of the Doomsday Bubble into the square, landing right in front of the Feldherrnhalle monument. The Bubble dominated the west side of the square, having overwhelmed the Theatine Church and surrounding structures. They gazed up at the monument – a large, exposed gallery (or loggia), which was built as a tribute to the Bavarian Army by King Ludwig I nearly 100 year earlier, though it had been updated a few times since then. It sheltered three big statues, with the largest being the central bronze, added in 1892, to commemorate the Franco-Prussian War and the unification of Germany. This statue featured a woman dressed in Roman-style robes holding a quill, alongside a naked soldier raising a flag, while standing over a relaxed lion. Two more prowling marble lions guarded the central staircase of the memorial.

Ronan turned to Chase. 'This can't be right. I thought we were aiming for night-time.'

Chase checked the Pod navigator. 'We're a day late. This is the closest instance of the Anomaly the navigator could find.'

'So we've missed the meeting? Damn! I was really looking forward to a beer.'

Chase turned to Beth. 'What does the book say?'

Beth pulled the book from her bag and flipped to the relevant section, but she knew the history of this day, it was a part of her heritage. 'After the initial coup things kind of fell apart, but Hitler decided to keep going, so the following day – today – they began their march on Berlin with about three thousand men. Statistically the odds aren't as good for us – they'll already have an influence on the future of the country – but the margin of probability is still in our favour.'

'So what do we do?'

'There's a clash with police in the city square. Hitler runs away but is later taken prisoner. That's when he writes Mein Kampf. Maybe we can intervene there.'

'Where's the city square?' Chase asked.

'I think we're in it,' Ronan said.

'Found them!' Aliyah pointed up a narrow side street – the Residenzstrasse – where Hitler could be seen leading a pack of 3,000 Nazi supporters out into the square. Most of the followers were civilians, though some were dressed in regular army uniform. Several of those in the front row wore the Nazi insignia on their sleeve and marched arm in arm, like a human barricade. Hitler wore a white coat making him stand out from the rest of the group.

Beth turned about. 'Oh, shit!'

The others followed her gaze and saw over a hundred armed Security Police (the *Sicherheitspolizei*) approaching rapidly across the square. They wore navy-blue uniforms with large silver buttons, black knee-high boots, and on top, a tall 'shako' (not quite a helmet, but more than a hat) that had the black, red and gold emblem of the Weimar Republic boldly emblazoned over the forehead. Some of the officers were on foot with pistols raised and ready to fire, others were on horseback with long spears poised like jousting spikes.

'Come on!' Caught in the middle with nowhere else to run, Ronan led the others up the staircase of the Feldherrnhalle monument. From here they had a spectacular view of the imminent clash. The police moved in quickly to try and block the rebels from entering the square.

'What now?' Aliyah asked as they watched from behind the statues.

Chase growled: 'We make sure Hitler dies.'

Adolph Hitler's rebel army spread out into the square, undaunted by the line of police. Adolph raised a pistol, firing a shot into the air. With a terrible cry the Nazis charged at the police. Across the square Senior Lieutenant Baron Michael von Godin raised his sabre and gave the command – 'Beriet! ... FEUER!'

The police fired on the charging rebels. Several of them dropped, dead or wounded. The Nazi rebels returned fire and two police officers were felled. Then the two sides collided. Chaos ensued.

The travellers watched in horror, while keeping an eye on the man in the white coat. Hitler was arm in arm with another man – war hero Max Erwin von Scheubner-Richter – when suddenly Max was shot and fell to the ground, dragging Adolph down with him.

Max lurched back up onto his feet and continued bravely, yelling something at the police as if daring them to shoot him down. Adolph meanwhile struggled to rise, and instead crawled away in retreat, dragging his right arm which had been dislocated. As he approached the Residenzstrasse from which they had come, he pulled himself to his feet and ran from the scene.

'He's getting away,' Ronan cried. 'Come on!'

Ronan leaped off the side of the monument down to the street, a drop of about two metres. The others followed, with Aliyah crouching into a roll and Beth and Chase climbing down quickly. Edmund, not used to such gymnastics, climbed down rather more slowly, and trailed after them.

They pursued the fleeing Hitler down the street while behind them the battle raged on. Adolph saw them giving chase. He pulled out his pistol to fire back at them, but the moment he raised his arm a world of pain shot through his shoulder and he screamed, dropping the gun on the street. He fled.

Beth had been fourth off the monument and while she tried to keep fit, she was not a runner. Nevertheless, she found herself flying past the others to take the lead in the chase. Thank God for practical shoes. Without missing a step, she snatched up the pistol from the ground and closed in on her prey.

Hitler emerged from the street into Max-Joseph-Platz square. This square also had a large statue overlooking it – Maximilian I, the first king of Bavaria, who sat on his throne likewise dressed in pseudo-Roman garb. King Maximillian watched dispassionately as Adolph Hitler ran into the square and made for a parked yellow convertible. The driver started the engine and opened the door for him. Hitler was about to get away.

A shot fired, hitting him in the back. Hitler fell hard.

In a panic the car sped away, the door slamming shut as it went.

Beth stepped out of the shadows, smoking pistol in her hand. She approached the wounded man lying on the street.

Hitler rolled over, blood soaking his white coat. He looked up at Beth as she stood over him, pointing his own pistol at his face. 'Jude...!'

Without hesitation Beth fired two more times, the report echoing down the narrow Munich streets. Hitler died instantly. There was a brief moment where the world stopped, at least for Beth. Time lost all meaning. Then, just as the others caught up with her, she dropped the pistol and walked away. 'Let's get the hell out of here.'

Beth led the way back up the Residenzstrasse. Aliyah chased after her. 'Beth. Are you okay?

"'Course, I'm okay.'

'I mean, you just killed a man.'

'If anyone deserved to die it was him.'

Aliyah nodded agreement. 'I really thought the 1920's would be more fun.'

Beth should have been offended, but Aliyah was an innocent, and you can't be angry with a child for speaking the truth.

Back in Odeonsplatz square, fourteen rebels and three police lay dead. The battle was all but over as police pursued the Nazi sympathisers up side-streets – leaving behind an eerie quiet, save for the remote echoes of scurried feet on stone pavements and occasional shots fired. Of those still in the square, some ran in a panic into the Anomaly, which was right where our travellers had left it.

'It didn't work,' Chase said.

'What?!'

Ronan sighed heavily. 'The Anomaly's still here. Nothing changed.'

They approached the growing Doomsday Bubble, which was now about to consume the Feldherrnhalle monument itself.

'You mean I killed Hitler for nothing? The war still happens?'

'Apparently so.'

Beth hit Chase. She was pissed. 'You said we could change the future. You promised!'

'I thought we could.'

She hit him again. Chase took it. 'But he's dead!' Beth cried. 'It has to change!'

'There is a greater power at work here, I think,' Edmund suggested.

Aliyah turned on Edmund. 'What? God? Fuck your God!?'

Edmund shrank. He was not used to such outspoken women. He wasn't sure he liked the future.

'Entropy,' Chase said quietly.

'Of course. Entropy,' Ronan echoed, not really understanding.

Chase explained. 'The universe is more resilient than we thought. If the change isn't big enough it just finds another way to bring that future about.'

'Killing Hitler wasn't a big enough change?!'

'Apparently not. It seems the probability of us inventing the time machine is very high. One could say, it's practically inevitable'.

'Sounds plausible,' Aliyah agreed sarcastically. 'As most wrong theories are.'

'Well that's... fucked,' Ronan protested. 'What are we supposed to do now?'

'We try again,' Beth said simply.

Chase looked at Beth, impressed by her resolve, and nodded. 'We have to go back further. That way the entropy over time will increase until the probability of us creating the time machine becomes virtually impossible. The more chaos we can create the better.'

Beth pulled out the book and started looking for another suitable moment in time to fuck with. 'We need to focus on big events. Things that will cause repercussions across generations.'

'By the time we're done, history won't recognize itself,' Ronan declared.

Edmund was shocked. 'That's a terrifying prospect,'

'Gotta be done.'

Beth found something. 'Okay, how about this? Jesus Christ.'

Edmund was horrified. 'You want to kill Jesus?!'

'I think we'll have better odds actually if we ensure Jesus never gets crucified and then, you know, raises from the dead. The whole Christian church is really built around that one event.'

Edmund was ecstatic. 'We're going to meet the saviour?'

'Why not?' Chase said. 'Let's go save Jesus.'

Meanwhile, across the square, Senior Lieutenant Baron Michael von Godin spotted the travellers standing near the giant unfathomable ball-thing, and called over a group of his men, led by Sergeant Hans Frimmel.

(They speak in German, of course, but I will translate here for the benefit of readers.)

'Who are they? Were they with the Nazi rebels?'

'I don't know, sir.'

'Arrest them, anyway.'

'But sir. They're right next to the Hell-Gate. Faust himself wouldn't dare to approach it.'

'Do as you're told, Sergeant!'

'Yes sir!' Frimmel led his men across the square towards the Hell-Gate and the strange travellers.

Chase finished entering the coordinates for their next destination into the Pod. 'All set.'

The travellers joined hands and prepared to walk into the Bubble.

'Halt! Sie sind festgenommen!' Frimmel ordered.

'Come on!' Ronan rushed forward pulling the others into the Anomaly after him.

While the other police wisely held back, fearful of the Hell-Gate, Sergeant Frimmel leaped forward and managed to grab onto Chase's arm – the one holding the Pod – just as he was pulled in. Frimmel was pulled in after them –

CHAPTER 9
Fuck the English

– Sergeant Hans Frimmel clung to Chase's right arm as the travellers tumbled about the vortex, dragged through time and space by the Pod gripped in Chase's hand. Chase and Frimmel eyeballed each other.

'Du bist verhaftet!' Frimmel commanded.

'I have no idea what you're saying!' Chase shouted back.

The travellers clung desperately to one another as they were flung to and fro by the turbulent eddies of the vortex. Chase tightened his grip on Beth's hand while at the same time trying to shake off the determined young Sergeant. But Frimmel had both hands wrapped around Chase's forearm; he was not about to let his prisoner escape.

Ronan, who was anchoring the other end of the human chain, tried to 'swim' around to help – 'Chase!... Chase!' – but the riptide was too strong.

Frimmel grabbed at the Pod sticking out from Chase's fist. Desperate not to lose the device, Chase released his grip from Beth and snapped his free hand over the Sergeant's. Chase and Frimmel tumbled away – both clinging to the Pod. The others flew off in the opposite direction.

'CHASE!!!' Ronan called franticly.

Beth turned to Aliyah. 'Look after yourself, kid.'

'What?!'

Beth releases her grip from Aliyah – '*No!*' – and flew towards Chase and Frimmel – '*BETH!*'

Beth crashed into a passing Spinosaurus, then bounced from that onto a decoratively saddled elephant from the army of Hannibal, which was promptly attacked in mid-flight by the Spinosaurus. Beth bounded off the elephant just in time to ricochet off a spinning satellite, bounce over a slab of the Titanic, and generally parkour her way across the debris of history until ultimately managing to grab hold of Chase's ankle.

'Beth!?'

'Us nerds gotta stick together!'

Chase, Frimmel and Beth fell out of the Vortex on their way to Jerusalem.

Ronan, Aliyah and Edmund fell out at a completely different place into –

– Guangzhou (known as the city of Canton to the English), China, 18th March, 1841. A Thursday. Ronan, Aliyah and Edmund tumbled from the Anomaly onto a narrow road paved with large stones and crowded by wood buildings up to four stories high – although the Anomaly had already destroyed the structures on one side of the road.

One of the buildings exploded, and the travellers ducked for cover under the awning of a nearby haberdashery as debris rained upon the street. Looking down the long avenue they spotted a nearby port. There was an armada of white-sailed tall ships firing cannons into the city or at the Chinese junks that floated nearby. The massive guns flashed, followed seconds later by a rumbling *boom*, and then a few seconds after that by the explosive collision of an iron cannonball with a nearby building. The ships were flying a British Union Jack flag, though some of them had red and white stripes not unlike a modern U.S.A flag.

'They're English!' Ronan declared.

'They're American!' Aliyah declared.

Among the vessels was an iron steamship called *Nemesis*. A direct hit from its guns caused a junk to explode in a blaze of kindling, smoke and human remains. Then, like the other ships, it directed its canon to fire into the city, the balls flying over the whitewashed warehouses that lined the port. The wooden structures burst into flaming shards, the fire quickly spreading into the heart of the city. People ran in a panic past the travellers, away from the port towards the safety of the city walls.

'Where the hell are we?!' Aliyah howled.

'China?' Ronan guessed based on the faces running past them.

'*When* the hell are we?!'

A contingent of soldiers emerged from the high-walled fort at the top of the road, marching towards them at double-pace. 'Maybe these guys can help. Hello?... Hello?! Can you tell us where we are?'

The Chinese commander yelled an order, and his men quickly surround the oddly dressed intruders, matchlock rifles shouldered and ready to fire, their fuses glowing in the smoke-filled air. The commander looked the strangers up and down, in particular Aliyah. He'd probably never seen a black woman before. He then pointed at the Anomaly. *'Is this some new weapon of yours? Do you intend to wipe us from the face of the earth?!'*

Ronan tried to reason with him. 'I'm sorry. I don't speak Chinese. I have no idea what you're saying.'

'*You are English?... English?*' Our travellers understood this word at least.

'Yes, English,' said Edmund proudly patting his chest.

'Irish, actually,' Ronan corrected, then pointed toward the harbour. 'Don't confuse me with that lot.'

'I'm American,' Aliyah said. 'Do you have Americans yet?'

'*Arrest them!*'

The travellers were grabbed, turned about, and their hands quickly bound with rope.

Edmund, as usual, was confused. 'What's happening?'

Ronan tried to reason with the commander. 'Hang on. I think there's been some kind of misunderstanding.'

'Maybe we should say we're Australian,' Aliyah suggested. 'Everyone likes Australians, right?'

'*You three, take them to the cells! The rest of you follow me.*'

'What did we do to upset them?' Edmund asked sincerely.

Three soldiers marched their prisoners back up the road into the fort, while the rest of the men double-timed it towards the battle.

The First Opium War was ostensibly about China stifling the trade of opium, which had been fostered decades earlier by the powerful East India Trading Company, and which was a tactic by the British to assert more control over what had been, until then, a healthy trade in silk, spices, and most importantly – tea. But as with most wars, it was really about money (in the form of silver), territory, and power. This was the day British forces attacked, and quickly took, the riverside suburbs of the city of Canton. Within two months, after a bloody siege, the British would breach the walls and claim the city as their own.

While the city endured bombardment by the far superior English cannons, Ronan, Edmund and Aliyah were thrown into a prison cell in one of the many forts that defended the city walls. They could hear the distant report of the guns from behind the thick stone walls.

'Great!' Aliyah kicked the door. 'Now what do we do?'

'I'm sure they'll let us go when they realize we're not a threat.' Edmund suggested innocently.

'By then the universe will be extinct!'

'Perhaps the others will have better luck with Jesus,' Edmund said.

A terrible thought occurred to Aliyah. She turned on Ronan. 'Explain something to me. What happens if Chase and Beth do succeed in changing the past enough so that you guys never create that thing? Will it just disappear?'

'That's the theory.'

'So how do we get home?'

Ronan hesitated. '... We don't.'

Aliyah was aghast.

Edmund was confused again. 'What about everyone that got caught up in this Doomsday Bubble of yours?'

'I guess when it goes, they're all stuck wherever they are at the time. Same as us.'

'So even if we stop this thing from destroying the entire universe, you've still managed to fuck up the entire history of everything.'

'Pretty much.'

'And we're trapped in a Chinese prison in the middle of a war zone,' – Aliyah checked her phone – 'with no cell coverage.'

'Could be worse...'

Aliyah hit Ronan – hard and repeatedly. 'How could this be any fucking worse?!'

'Ow! Ow! Stop it!'

'What the hell were you thinking!?' HIT HIT HIT!

'Chase built it! Hit him!'

'If he was here I would!' HIT HIT HIT!!

Ronan ran around the cell to escape Aliyah's wrath. Edmund tried to restrain her as gently as he could, 'Aliyah, please. This isn't helping,' then he copped an elbow in the face for his efforts.

'No. But it feels good. Stupid fucking crelboin!' HIT HIT HIT HIT!!!

Edmund finally managed to pull Aliyah away, but not before she got in one last HIT at Ronan's head. She sat in the corner, fuming, while Ronan rubbed himself all over.

Edmund, suddenly the voice of reason, stood between them. 'Attacking one another will not help our mission. We need to devise a plan of escape.'

'If we had a Pod we could get out of here easy.' Aliyah addressed Ronan: 'Sure you don't have one shoved up your arse?'

'Please,' Edmund pleaded. 'There's no need for vulgarity.'

'I think I might know where we are?' Ronan speculated.

'No shit, Sherlock – *China*.'

'No, I mean, *when* we are. I think this is one of the Opium Wars.'

'One of them?'

'There were three. I don't know much about them, but I do know it's how England got Hong Kong, and they kind of decimated the Chinese in the process. It was English imperialism at its best. Or worst. Depending which side you're on.'

'Well, the English of course,' Edmund said automatically.

Aliyah agreed. 'I mean, if the Chinese are pushing opium on the world, then – '

'– No,' Ronan interrupted. 'No, it's the other way round. The English got the Chinese hooked on opium so they could buy more tea.'

'What the fuck?'

'That can't be right,' Edmund argued. 'You must be remembering it wrong.'

'No. That much I'm sure of,' Ronan searched his memory. 'Yes. It was the East India Company – they started it, I think. But the British government got involved and the whole thing turned into a massive scam on the Chinese. Basically, ended imperial China.'

'Excuse me, but what is opium?' Edmund asked.

'It's a drug,' Aliyah said. 'A very powerful drug.'

'A drug?'

'Jeeze, you really didn't get out much in the Middle Ages, did you?' Aliyah took Edmund by the hand. 'Imagine … a bottle of wine – you had wine, yes? – imagine a wine that got you so drunk you forgot who you were, or where you were, and the moment you got sober you had to do it again, so you were basically always drunk. And you would waste away and eventually die, and you wouldn't even care.'

Edmund turned white. 'That sounds horrible.'

'Yeah. It is.' Aliyah sat back down, suddenly quiet.

Ronan sensed the rapid change in Aliyah's mood. 'You okay?'

'Yeah. But… you know… Fuck the English. Sorry Edmund.'

'Yeah,' Ronan echoed with his Northern Irish cadence. 'Fuck the English.'

Edmund stood before them defiantly. 'Do not count me among those who would do such a thing. I would not trade on the lives of others for mere profit. So… fuck them.'

Aliyah smiled – the corruption of Edmund had begun.

Meanwhile – in the Garden of Gethsemane, on Wednesday, April 1 in the year 33 (yes, April Fool's day). Although, the garden was really more of an olive grove, with stout olive trees set in neat rows, and a well-trod path running through them with occasional wooden benches for visitors to relax and meditate. In the centre of the grove was a small clearing. This was where Chase, Beth and Sergeant Frimmel found the disciples of Jesus sleeping – curled up on the patchy grass or leaning against the potholed trees. A couple of them were snoring.

'Okay. So which one's Jesus?' Beth asked softly.

'I don't think here's here,' Chase whispered. 'I only count eleven.'

'One's missing.'

'Probably Judas.'

Beth nodded. 'Right.' Even though she was not Christian, Beth knew the story well enough. Aliyah had made her sit through the film of *Jesus Christ Superstar* several times; she wanted to play Judas.

Since emerging from the Hell-Gate, Sergeant Frimmel, confused and somewhat at a loss for what to do next, tried talking to his 'prisoners', but they didn't speak German, so he eventually went quiet and just followed after them – they seemed to know where they were going. The bafflement of the Hell-Gate and this strange new place confounded him, such that his brash police officer front had withered away and he reverted to the apprehensive young man he was when out of uniform; so he tagged along, hoping they would eventually enlighten him on their situation, and lead him back home.

Chase looked at Frimmel. In his navy-blue police uniform he stuck out like …well, like a cop for one thing. But also like a cop from the future. Chase called up the Pod interface and selected the *Holo Outfitter* function. He pointed the device at one of the sleeping disciples. The Pod 'sampled' the clothes the man was wearing, creating a digital replica. Chase then pointed the Pod at Frimmel. His German police uniform was 'wrapped' in a holographic identikit of the disciple's clothes, rendering a completely realistic and perfectly fitted set of robes on Frimmel. He looked like a local – except for the shako, which remained on his head, and the toes of his boots poking out from under the virtual robes.

Frimmel was astonished.

'How did you do that?' Beth asked.

'It's just a holo-projection. I figured it would be good for trying on clothes.'

Frimmel touched his robed arm. His hand went right through the 'cloth', disturbing the projection and revealing his uniform underneath. As he removed his hand the hologram restored.

'Is this some kind of magic trick?' Frimmel asked.

Chase shook his head, not as an answer, but because he couldn't understand the Sergeant. He repeated the process, creating holo-clothes for Beth and himself. All three now appeared to be wearing robes of the era 'copied' from the sleeping disciples.

'Excuse me, sir. But are you a magician?'

Chase scrolled through the settings on the Pod display and selected the translator. 'Say again.'

'Are you a magician?' Frimmel said in perfect English.

'No. Just a scientist.' Chase answered.

'You speak German!'

'He's speaking English!' Beth said.

'And *you* speak German!'

Chase shushed them both. Then explained quietly, 'It's the translator.'

'But how is it doing that?' Beth asked. 'It's in real time, and the sound is coming out of our mouths.'

'It's just a phase transfer function, with a bit of predictive AI.'

'Like a ventriloquist,' Beth suggested.

Chase frowned. 'No, not like a ventriloquist.'

'Are you both speaking English now?' Frimmel was confused. 'I only hear German.'

'Yeah, that's just another phase trick, it cancels the original voice out, so you only hear the translation.'

'Like the TARDIS in Doctor Who,' Beth postulated.

'No.'

'Or like a live movie dub.'

Chase frowned again. 'No.'

'You like the movies?' Frimmel asked Beth excitedly.

'Sure. I like movies.'

'What are your favourite movies? I especially like the films of Fritz Lang and Charlie Chaplin.'

'I don't know them,' Beth admitted. 'A bit before my time, I'm afraid.'

Frimmel grabbed Beth enthusiastically. 'Buster Keaton!'

Chase shushed. 'Keep it down.'

Frimmel shrank. 'Sorry… I love movies. I am Frimmel, by the way. Hans Frimmel.'

'Chase. Beth. Now be quiet.'

Frimmel nodded vigorously, then said in a quiet aside to Beth, accompanied by creepy finger gestures: 'Nosferatu.'

'Come on,' Chase waved. 'He can't be far away.'

Leaving the disciples to their slumber, they roamed the garden in search of Jesus. Beth pulled out her smartphone (an iPhone X) and showed it to Frimmel. 'You like movies? Check this out.' She filmed a short clip of Frimmel.

'What is it?'

She played the clip back for him *'What is it?'*

'Oh. My. God. It is a movie camera!? But it's so small.'

'Have a go. Just press the red button.'

Frimmel filmed Beth, then panned around to film Chase. Beyond him was another man walking alone among the olive trees, deep in contemplation.

'Is that him?' Beth asked Chase.

'Has to be.'

'He looks very … Jewish,' Beth was unimpressed. He was just a guy. Though admittedly a rather attractive one, with a swarthy complexion, dark hair and piercing brown eyes.

Meanwhile, Frimmel filmed their conversation.

'So what now?' Beth asked.

'We kidnap him before Judas gets back.'

'And do what? Hold him for ransom?'

Chase was making this up as he went along. 'We just need to make sure he's not arrested. Then he can't be tried. And if he's not tried, he won't be crucified.'

'That'll just delay the inevitable,' Beth reasoned. 'I think we need to take him out – permanently.'

Chase was shocked, 'You want me to kill Jesus!?'

'*Noooo*. We take him back through the bubble. To some other time.'

'Oh.'

Frimmel was still trying to catch up. 'Where exactly are we?'

'Are you filming this?" Chase asked.

Frimmel lowered the phone. 'No.'

'Actually, that's a good idea. Keep filming. We're making history here, after all.'

Frimmel raised the phone back up.

'Better yet. You're a policeman. Go arrest that man.'

'Why? Is he a Nazi?'

'Yes.'

Frimmel hesitated. 'You said he was Jesus.'

'Different Jesus.'

'I think we should just go talk to him,' Beth reasoned.

Chase conceded. 'Okay. But keep your gun handy, Sergeant. Just in case.'

Frimmel nodded. He felt better when there were clear orders to follow.

Beth took the lead as they stepped out from their cover. 'Hello.'

Jesus, who had been deep in contemplation, turned to receive the three strangers, noting the odd shiny stick held by one, and the odd headpiece worn by the one holding up a small tablet. His eyes landed on Beth. 'Hello.'

'Are you Jesus?' Beth asked.

Confusion. 'My name is Yeshua. Yeshua Ben Yoseph.'

Beth nodded. 'Of course. Would you mind coming with us?'

'I was expecting Judah.'

'Judah will betray you.'

'I know.'

There was a brief silence as no-one quite knew what to say next. Frimmel moved around to get a better shot.

'We can protect you,' Chase said.

Yeshua smiled benevolently. 'Thank you, but events are already in motion. I think it best to let things take their course.'

'We can take you away from here, to somewhere no one will ever find you.'

'This has already been suggested – to take me across the sea, to Gallia or Britannia. But why would I run? My life is here.'

'And you'll die here, very soon, if you don't come with us now,' Chase argued.

Yeshua placed a hand on Chase's shoulder, his holo-robes glitching at the touch. Yeshua pulled away, puzzled. 'I appreciate your concern, brother. But we must each follow our own path. Mine is here. If I am to die, then there is nothing you or anyone else can do about it.'

Chase hesitated, briefly entranced the man's charisma. Then, shaking himself out of it: 'The hell with that. Sergeant!'

Frimmel, still filming with one hand, drew his luger and aimed it at Yeshua, who looked upon the gun with a bold curiosity. 'Is that a weapon of some sort?' He turned to Chase. 'You threaten to kill me, in order to save me from death.' Then to Beth. 'Sister. You know this will not work.'

'But we have to try.'

With Frimmel's pistol aimed at his back, Yeshua went with them willingly. They left the garden and after a twenty-minute walk came to the Anomaly, which had overwhelmed the city walls and half the Temple of Jerusalem.

'What is that?' Yeshua asked, genuinely astonished.

'The end of days,' Beth told him.

'So soon.'

With Beth leading the way, they walked into the Anomaly.

CHAPTER 10
The Four Treasures

Aliyah was singing *Waiting for the End of the World* by Elvis Costello. Her voice reverberated off the cold stone walls of their prison cell like a ghostly chorus. Ronan and Edmund had long since given up trying to dissuade her from singing. It was Aliyah's way of dealing with stress, and they preferred a calm Aliyah. Plus, she was a pretty good singer. Excellent, in fact. In the past several hours she had worked her way through the scores of several musicals, occasionally belting out a big showstopper like *Rose's Turn, Cabaret* or *Heaven on their Minds,* then balancing this with a ballad like *My House, Children Will Listen* or *Moving On.* Once she had mined her Musical Theatre repertoire, she began singing pop songs from the likes of Beyonce, Whitney Houston and The Spice Girls, steadily going backwards in time through the twenty-tens, the noughties, the nineties, and was now digging into more obscure New Wave songs from the 1980's. Her musical knowledge was quite remarkable for someone so young – the benefit of a Spotify education.

Aliyah's song was interrupted by the cell door bursting open and a burly Chinese guard barking orders at them. He barked again, then, realizing they didn't speak Chinese, jerked his head for them to follow him out.

Surrounded by a contingent of soldiers (they really weren't taking any chances with these English prisoners) the travellers were led up the narrow stone staircases of the fort, across the grounds of the inner city and into the palace. Here, they were marched into a spacious, cold stone room with a large table surrounded by chairs. They were '*told*' to sit and wait. Aliyah tried asking the others what they thought was going on but was quickly silenced by the guard.

So, they waited …

Eventually a door opened somewhere, and a slow shuffling could be heard approaching. In time, a very old man appeared slowly making his way across the stone floor, followed discretely by a younger man (younger, that is, by contrast; he was in his fifties) carrying a large bag. The old man had a long white beard and his long white hair was tucked into a neat ponytail. He wore the simple black pants and shirt of a Chinese officer, though with a black and red *guanmao* hat upon his head, signalling his rank as an official of the Emperor. The younger old man wore a simple black skull cap over hair not yet fully white and with a short grey beard. After several minutes of excruciating shuffling, the old man gingerly sat himself at the head of the table. The younger man stood by, coiled, in case aid was required, but otherwise kept a respectful distance. Despite his age and seeming infirmity, once settled in his chair the old man was alert and imposing – the kind who had fought many battles and survived to tell the tale. Now that he was settled, the aide relaxed and moved to the side, maintaining his respectful distance.

The old man looked at each of the prisoners in turn – Edmund, Ronan, and Aliyah. Like the commander from earlier his eyes dwelled on Aliyah curiously. They didn't get many young black women in Canton, and certainly not ones dressed quite so theatrically.

Eventually the old man mumbled something to his aide, who produced from his bag several blank sheets of rice paper and laid them on the table in two neat piles. He weighed the sides on each pile down with small rectangular turquoise slabs. He then produced two ivory handled brushes, and two black inksticks with ornate gold designs etched around their sides. Next to these he placed a circular black inkslab made of stone, a small white bowl, and then a smaller white bowl with an elaborate blue pattern painted around it, along with a matching porcelain stand. From a flask he poured some water into the white bowl. He dipped the two brushes into the water and let them soak for a while, occasionally taking them out to test and pinch the tips. After a couple of minutes, he groomed the brushes on a soft cloth to remove the excess water, pinched their tips to a fine point and placed them in the little porcelain stand. He then poured some water into the smaller ornate white bowl, and with a tiny silver spoon, carefully scooped out a couple of drops of water and placed these in the centre of the inkslab. Taking one of the inksticks he dipped the end in the water, let it sit for a moment as it soaked in the moisture, and then began to swirl it around the flat surface of the slab, gently grinding out a paste of black ink. This took about two minutes. Setting the inkstick aside, he then nodded to the old man that the four treasures were ready for use, and the aide returned to his place at the old man's side. This whole process had taken around ten minutes to complete.

The old man took up one of the brushes and with masterful calligraphy, painted out some characters on the paper set before him. He then pulled this sheet off the pile and handed it to his aide. The aide read it aloud, translating into perfect English: 'I am General Yang Fang. Representative of his Imperial Majesty the Emperor of the Great Qing Dynasty, Son of Heaven, Lord of Ten Thousand Years, and leader of the imperial forces in Guangzhou.' The aide swallowed, then said: 'Now who the hell are you?'

After so long a silence each of the three travellers momentarily forgot how to talk. Several seconds passed, then General Yang banged his fist on the table and yelled at them, '*Nǐ shì shéi!*'

'Oh, well, I'm Ronan, this is Edmund –'

'– Good evening, sir –'

'– and this is Aliyah.'

'– Hi.'

'We were just kind of … passing through, you know. We're not with those folk on the ships. I'm Irish actually.'

'I'm Australian,' Aliyah offered.

'I regret to say that I am English,' Edmund admitted, 'but I do not condone the actions of my fellow countrymen –'

'Fuck the English!' Aliyah declared.

'– I am from a far more civilised time,' Edmund explained calmly.

'Trust me, we're not with them,' Ronan said, waving in the general direction of where he thought the port was. The others agreed and soon all three were talking over each other trying to explain how much they were not on the side of the English aggressors.

Eventually the 'young' aide raised his hand and they fell silent. He then took up the brush and painted some characters onto the second stack of paper set before him. The general watched as he did so, confusion turning to anger then turning back around to confusion. He snatched the sheet off the stack, crushed it into and ball and threw it aside. Taking the brush from his aide he dashed another set of characters on the paper before him and handed this sheet to his aide.

'Then tell us how to defeat this terrible new weapon the English have.'

Ronan had to think for a moment, then he recalled the iron warship they had seen decimate one of the Chinese junks. 'You mean the *Nemesis*? Ah, sure. We can probably help you with that.'

The aide looked confused. He dashed off a translation. The General dashed another response. 'No, the General means the gigantic sphere that is destroying the city.'

'Oh, that's not theirs,' Ronan blurted. Aliyah shushed him.

This slip did not go unnoticed by the aide, who clearly knew more about the behaviour of western barbarians than his present duties revealed. 'Why is it attacking our city?' he asked unprompted.

'It's not. Well… it is. But… it's just doing what gigantic apocalyptic spheres do.'

'We call it the Doomsday Bubble,' Edmund intoned glumly.

'Are you responsible for this Doomsday Bubble?' The aide asked Edmund, who promptly shook his head and pointed at Ronan.

The aide glared at Ronan, who screwed up his face and offered feebly, 'We're trying to fix it – I mean, get rid of it.' Then more confidently, 'In fact, if we help you defeat the English, that might also get rid of the … sphere.'

The aide held up a finger to pause the conversation, then wrote down what had been said for the General.

'What are you telling him?' Aliyah asked.

'Just that you have offered to help us defeat the English and destroy *all* of their weapons.' He handed the sheet to General Yang, who, upon reading the contents of the page smiled, nodded, and grunted assent.

Meanwhile, in the Haight-Ashbury district of San Francisco in the summer of '67, Chase, Beth, Frimmel and Yeshua Ben Yoseph strolled down Haight away from the Anomaly, which had unfortunately overwhelmed the Filmore and Geary Boulevarde, and was encroaching on Lafayette Park to the north and Alamo Square in the south. But for now, the famed centre of the city with its Victorian era four-storey painted lady terraces and their curved turrets and brownstone stairs remained untouched. As did the drugstores, diners, barbers and jewellers, tattoo parlours, fruit shops, TV stores, cleaners, real estate brokers, and glass storefronts adorned with psychedelic poster art for local music venues and bands like *The Jefferson Airplane* or *The Grateful Dead*. The place smelled of tobacco and car exhaust, with notes of eucalyptus and camphor acne cream mixed with the ambiguous aroma of incense and weed.

'Are you sure about this,' Chase asked Beth as passers-by gave them odd looks.

'Trust me. He'll fit right in. Where better to hide a rebel pacifist than in the counter-culture of the 1960's. He just needs to join some folk-rock band writing songs about peace and love and no-one will think twice.' While Beth's logic may have been correct in principle, they were nevertheless eye-catching in their various attires, for the diversity of said counter-culture which presently surrounded them made everyone look conspicuously normal. Some of the men had longer hair and beards than those of another age might, and a few people were dressed colourfully in ochres and browns and earthy reds, but mixed in with these outliers were jeans and t-shirts, corduroy and crimplene, business suits with collars and ties, overalls, stripes and checks, bare feet, moccasin and leather shoes, headbands, top hats, bowlers and andy caps, cardigans and blouses, short skirts, single-piece dresses and kimonos, leather jackets and khaki vests. There were so many styles that no one 'look' could be said to define the time and place, despite what movies and later tourist outlets would have us believe. And despite there being a massive Anomaly eating the city to the north, everyone seemed implacably calm. Haight-Ashbury remained its own little world, oblivious to what was happening just a few blocks away.

Yeshua looked as if he'd stepped out of a nativity scene, so he fit right in with the eclectic style of the time – odd, but somehow befitting. Beth and Chase in their more formal suits simply looked like uptown squares passing through. Frimmel, on the other hand, in his German police uniform did not fit in at all; and holding a shiny flat brick to his face as he walked didn't help. Chase quickly sampled a passer-by's pants, shirt and jacket and 'dressed' Frimmel more in keeping with their new surroundings. He lifted the shako from Frimmel's head.

'What are you doing?'

'You can't wear this here.'

'It is part of my uniform. I must.'

Chase discretely left the Shako on an outdoor fruit stand among the oranges. 'We'll pick it up on the way back,' he lied. 'Besides, it gets in the way of your filming.'

Frimmel accepted this argument. It was a necessary sacrifice.

The one thing that made our party of time travellers stand out more than their anachronistic clothes, was their pace. They strolled, while those around them practically dashed. Everyone, it seemed, was intent on being somewhere else, each walking with purpose and resolve. Aside from a couple of substance-influenced rakes who wandered aimlessly back and forth, their blank stares more disconcerting than confronting, everyone was cheerfully determined. This was not a place to just 'hang out' or 'be seen'. It was a place of transition. A place that got you from where you were to where you wanted to be. How much of this inspired mobility amounted to anything real was something each person would each discover for themselves within the next year or so; but for now, the mood was electric, and no news bulletin about a carnivorous bubble somewhere uptown was about to distract them from their purpose.

Yeshua drew the most attention, not just because of his impressive robes and charismatic bearing, but because he looked so much like a man on a mission, and even had his own small entourage to boot. He was the archetype hippie as portrayed on the front cover illustration of the newsletter – *The Oracle* – which was prominently displayed in several storefronts, portraying the symbolic figure of the Aquarian Age human as a long-haired bearded angel, dressed in classic robes, arms outstretched (crucifix-like) holding up two enormous bongs trailing smoke and unicorns. It was as if Yeshua had personally posed for the picture.

'Is that supposed to be me?' Yeshua asked when he saw the image.

'I don't think so,' Beth said. 'But it's a good sign, don't you think?'

'Perhaps. But a sign of what exactly?'

'Are you in a band?' a passing stranger with a guitar slung over his back asked Yeshua.

Yeshua was confused. 'A band?'

'You guys look like a band.'

'No,' Chase answered. 'We're not a band.'

The young guitarist looked Yeshua in the eye. 'You wanna be?'

'I don't know,' Yeshua said. 'What is it?'

'We're called *The Starfish Explosion,* though I might change that if we think of something better. Kind of blues-rock with a bit of a soul. We're still workin' it out. But we need a singer. Do you sing?'

'Everyone can sing.'

'Yeah. Right on. I figured you for a front man the moment

I saw you. You got that pizzaz, you know? Star quality.' The young man took out a small notepad, flipped past some pages of what appeared to be poetry or lyrics, and started writing on a blank page with a pencil. 'Come on by the house, man. We can jam and, you know, see if any sparks fly.'

'Sparks?'

'Yeah. Try out some ideas. Hang out. Have some food. Smoke some pot. Who knows? Maybe start a revolution. At the very least you'll meet some nice people and get a free meal. You're all welcome,' he told the others as he tore the page out and handed the address to Yeshua.

'Thank you.'

'You know who you remind me of, man? Jim Morrison. You know, from *The Doors*. Only like, more so. Anyone ever tell you that?'

'I don't know who that is,' Yeshua confessed.

The guitarist smiled knowingly. 'Yeah. LA band, right? Love the look by the way. Very cool. Though maybe add some leather. You'd look good in leather. But we can talk about that. See you tonight, yeah?' And with that the stranger left them.

'People here seem a lot friendlier than in Jerusalem,' Yeshua noted.

Meanwhile, in 19th century Guangzhou, Ronan, Aliyah and Edmund were devising a plan to defeat the English forces that were besieging the city, and hopefully turn history on its head. The big problem (aside from the ever-growing Anomaly) was the warship *Nemesis*. If they could take out that vessel the Chinese stood a much better chance of victory over the English (*Fuck the English!*).

The 'young' aide who had served as their translator with General Yang Fang was named Liang Fa. He was a native of Guangdong province, having lived most of his life in Gaungzhou (*Canton*). His name meant 'he who is sent', and indeed, he seemed to have been sent by providence to be in this place at this time. He was an early convert to protestant Christianity and therefore sympathetic to westerners, and lived a precarious life as a result. Nevertheless, his skills as a translator for the foreign barbarians had saved him more than once.

Through Liang Fa the travellers discovered the British now controlled most of *Canton*, their flags again flying over the dockside factories. But the walled part of the city and various forts along the rivers remained uncaptured. The British commander was a man by the name of George Elliot, who had offered a truce. Elliot wanted a peaceful resolution and for trade to continue. It was not the first time he has suggested such a truce. Just a few weeks earlier an agreement had been made between Elliot and the former Chinese commander Qishan, which included the surrender of the islands known as Hong Kong (*Heung Gong* or '*Fragrant Harbour*'). Despite these efforts, neither side accepted the deal and hostilities resumed. Qishan was promptly replaced by Yang Fang, who had many years of experience but was old and deaf – hence the whole business with the written translations.

Liang Fa, despite his western sympathies, hated the opium trade and thought the present war was grossly misguided, and that it would turn the Chinese people away from Christianity. He and Edmund found an instant rapport. They both loved the English, but hated what they were doing.

('Fuck the English!' Aliyah repeated every time their name was mentioned.)

More importantly, both Edmund and Liang Fa were devout Christians.

'But you are Catholic, yes?' Liang Fa asked.

'Of course.'

'I was taught in the protestant tradition, specifically presbyterian.'

'I don't know what that is.' Edmund's faith came 500 years before Martin Luther.

'We are mortal enemies,' Liang Fa told him dispassionately. 'At least, that is how most Westerners see it.'

'Why?'

'I don't fully understand it myself. Something to do with the Pope, I think?'

'But you still believe in Christ the saviour?' Edmund asked.

'Yes, indeed.'

'Then that's all that matters.'

There were 30,000 Chinese soldiers camped just outside the city, with more on the way. Admiral Elliot had promised to withdraw his men if the new truce was signed, and Liang Fa knew him to be a man of honour – even if his superiors back in London were not. This would give the Chinese time to prepare a retaliatory assault, or at least a better defence. Meanwhile the travellers could do something no Chinese man could do – infiltrate the English forces as one of them.

It was decided Ronan and Edmund would dress in the uniforms of captured soldiers (the Chinese had had *some* small successes, after all), travel into occupied territory down by the river and sabotage as many ships as they could. Meanwhile Aliyah ('*Fuck the English!*') would help with the assault that was to follow. (It was gently argued, of course, that a young black woman whose military experience amounted to a regional production of *Hair,* or having sat through *Rambo* more than once because it had been her boyfriend's favourite movie, wouldn't be readily accepted by a 19th century Chinese army as a credible advisor, but Aliyah began singing *My Shot* from *Hamilton* so everyone just let her have her way.)

Ronan and Edmund drove a horse-drawn cart down the cobbled streets of Canton, into English occupied territory outside the city walls. The cart was laden with porcelain melons – basically two circular bowls placed one atop the other. These were normally used to transport balls of opium and were instantly recognisable to anyone working at the Thirteen Factories district alongside the Pearl River. These buildings were not actually factories, but the trading posts, warehouses and residences for all foreign merchants who bought and sold goods to mainland China. Each 'factory' was run by a different country or organisation, such as the East India Company.

Western merchants were normally restricted to this 'golden ghetto', which was a pleasant place to live and work; not just because of the modern western architecture (at least on the outside), but also the courtyard gardens that extended down to the riverbank which had tall trees, flower beds and a prominent flagpole flying the colours of the home country.

But that was in the best of times. The factories, while not completely ruined, were burned, their fences uprooted, and the gardens trampled – victims of the Chinese assault that had begun the war. Despite this, trade continued – especially in opium. Even war could not stop the engine of commerce for long; and no one stopped Ronan and Edmund's cart as they drove past the checkpoints with a friendly wave. Business as usual. The diplomatic division between the factories had dissolved as all the Western merchants rallied to make the best of a bad situation, so two soldiers transporting opium to the docks was not to be questioned. In fact, it was encouraged, as one guard offered to help them transfer their cargo from the cart into a rowboat.

'You're Irish,' their helper commented when he heard Ronan's accent.

'Yeah, what of it?'

'My Mam's Irish. Galway. Where you from?'

'Kinevarra,' Ronan lied, knowing it wasn't far from Galway.

'Ah! Just over the water! What are you doin' here?'

'I could ask the same of you.'

'Yeah. See the world! And now that I'm here all I want to do is get back home.'

'Yeah. Me too,' Ronan said, and meant it.

The guard then helped them load the buckets of pitch onto the boat. 'What you need this for?'

'To make repairs. You know, in case any of the Chinese cannons actually hit one of our ships.' Ronan had prepared what to say in case he got just such a question.

'Yeah, right. Gotcha. Good luck with it, then.'

'Cheers.'

'What?'

'…Farewell friend. Thanks for the help.'

With Edmund at the oars they quickly pulled away, their helper waving cheerfully after them until they vanished into the gloom of the unlit bay.

Aliyah sat with Liang Fa in an opulent anteroom not far from where they had first met – quite a difference from the cell they had been thrown in just the day before.

'So, you're not from Australia. You're from the Americas,' Liang Fa repeated, curious.

'United States.'

'And you are a free woman.'

'Of course!' Aliyah blurted; then remembered where – and when – she was.

Liang Fa was unfazed. 'We did away with slavery two hundred years ago. The Emperor Shengzu outlawed it. Didn't see the value in it.'

'Hmm. We'll get there eventually. Might have to fight a war to do it, though.'

'Here in Canton,' he used the English name since they were speaking English, 'the practice persists, despite the prohibition. That, and the opium trade, are two things about the English that are difficult to abide.'

'Your English is very good,' Aliyah said.

'Thank you. I had a good teacher.'

'Why did you become a Christian?' Aliyah asked bluntly.

This one fazed Liang Fa just a little. 'I was young, and admired a missionary named Robert Morrison. But my faith is genuine. And I still honour the teachings of Confucius.'

'Isn't that … like … a conflict of interest?'

Liang Fa took a moment to grasp what she meant. 'Not at all. Confucius was a great teacher, but not a god. The Christ was both.'

Aliyah could have pushed back on that, but didn't want to offend her host, so she let it slide; instead changing the subject back to the real purpose of this meeting: 'I have an idea that might help. With your soldiers.'

Liang Fa raised an eyebrow. It reminded Aliyah of Mister Spock from *Star Trek*.

'Do you play music during a battle … you know, to gee the men up?'

'We have drums.'

'That's good. But you could do more. Got any songs? Like anthems that can inspire the men?'

'We have many songs…but not of the kind you are thinking. You mean like *God Save the King*?'

Aliyah wavered. '…Yes. But better.'

'What did you have in mind?'

Meanwhile, in 1967 San Francisco, Chase, Beth, Frimmel and Yeshua arrived at the address they had been given. It was one of those multi-storied painted lady terraces, the heart of west coast bohemia and the 60's counter-culture. The front door was wide open, delivering The Beatles sitar and flange infused *Norwegian Wood* mingled with the beguiling odours of pseudo-Indian/Asian/American foods. On entering, after a short walk down a long hall, they discovered a spacious living room with threadbare shawls tacked over the tall windows to diffuse the harsh daylight, music festival and band posters sticky taped to the walls, a vast record collection piled in haphazard order against one wall, middling American flags presented like a bouquet of flowers over the old fireplace, and a weary Persian rug not quite obscuring the flaking wooden floorboards, held in place by fat old sofas covered in colourful blankets to hide the holes. It was anachronistically charming and thoroughly anarchic in a naïve, conformist kind of way. A record player, the source of the music, was spinning away in one corner, plugged into a guitar amp for added volume.

Sitting on the fat old sofas, or on hard wooden chairs, or draped on the Persian rug, was an equally anachronistic group of 'hippies' dragging on bongs or joints, the smoke rising to and drifting across the high ceiling in psychedelic eddies. That explained one of the beguiling odours that infused with the food smells emanating from the kitchen at the back of the house. It also explained the protracted nature of the conversations taking place, as if time had slowed to a crawl and couldn't be bothered getting up when company arrived because it was too busy pontificating about the cosmic significance of a D Minor 7th chord.

Yeshua smiled. 'Kaneh-bosem,'

'We call it cannabis these days,' Beth explained. 'Or marijuana.'

Frimmel was turning green. 'I feel sick.'

"You came!' The guitarist who had invited them emerged from one of the sofas and stumbled towards them. He wrapped his arm around Yeshua's shoulder. "Everybody! This is the guy I was telling you about. The singer! What was your name again?'

'Yeshua.'

'Yeshua!! Yes, you are! I'm Mike. Mike Bloomfield. Let's jam!' Then handing his joint to Beth: 'Please, sit. Enjoy.'

Beth immediately passed the joint on to Chase, who considered it for a moment, figured *what the hell*, and took a puff.

Frimmel sat on the rug and tried not to throw up. But he kept filming on Beth's iPhone…

Less than a minute later electric guitars, amplifiers, saxophones and trumpets had been pulled from their cases and were wielded – ready to rock. A mic was plugged into one of the guitar amps and handed to Yeshua (*a Sonotone CM10A for those taking note of such things*).

Mike started playing a lick and the band quickly picked up

the groove – an up-tempo 12-bar blues. They were just improvising but already it sounded incredible. Chase was getting into it, head nodding. Beth's foot started tapping involuntarily, though just the foot – nothing else. Frimmel was alarmed and covered his ears. Yeshua, still clutching the microphone, was astonished, excited, and a little confused.

'Just sing something!' Mike called to him. 'Anything!'

Yeshua raised the mic to his lips, started nodding to the music and began to sing:

'Hear O Israel,
The Lord is our God, the Lord is one.
And as for you, you shall love the Lord your God
With all your heart,
With all your soul,
And with all of your strength.'

It was the ancient prayer of Shema. Beth recognised it immediately. It was a prayer all devout Jews knew since it was sung twice a day as part of one's morning and evening rituals. It was quite simply the first thing that occurred to Yeshua to sing. He was singing in his native Hebrew, but Chase's translator turned it instantly into English as it had been doing for all of Yeshua's utterances. However, it was not sung exactly as one would normally sing it. Yeshua found a way to make it work with the blues riff being played, making it sound more like a Gospel/Soul testimony straight out of the Mississippi Delta. On repeating the prayer, the horns spontaneously picked up on the rhythm and punctuated the '*with all's*' with a series of staccato blasts, kicking the song into high gear.

Yeshua just kept on singin' the prayer, and with each round became more and more inspired by the music until he was wailing at the sky, the microphone distorting his voice in that perfect way only a cheap microphone plugged into a guitar amp can. Everyone was on their feet dancing. The music drifting out the open door into the street where a crowd soon gathered with strangers entering the house and straining to see who was playing, and who on earth was singing like they were about to tear the roof off the house and the sky off the world. It was magnificent. He sounded like Elvis, Sam Cooke, and Joe Cocker all rolled into one glorious tenor affirmation of life.

As Chase, Beth and Frimmel left the party and moved out of range, the singing reverted to Hebrew; but by then no-one cared about the words – if they ever did. It was the voice that mattered. The voice that would debut at Monterey Pop Festival just a few months later and set the world on fire. The voice that would go on to sell a million records, inspire the hearts and souls of millions of fans around the world, and convince Mike Bloomfield to not dabble with heroin and other hard drugs, and survive to live a long, fruitful life as one of the greatest guitarists of all time.

Meanwhile, in 1841 Guangzhou, under cover of night, Ronan and Edmund rowed alongside each English vessel they encountered and attached a time-bomb to its hull. The devices were devised by Ronan using a Chinese thunder-crash bomb (a primitive grenade), along with the flint from a flintlock rifle (these were mostly captured weapons – the Chinese were still using matchlocks), connected to a chronometer as the timer, and all packaged up inside the porcelain opium bowls. These were then bound together with bamboo strips, covered with pitch, and stuck to the hull of the ship. They had made about fifty of the devices, not enough to sink every ship of the English fleet (there were close to 200 spread across the Pearl

River and its tributaries), but enough to cripple the big ones. They reserved four of the bombs for *The Nemesis*. Each bomb was set to go off at 6am, just before sunrise. That gave them about nine hours, an average of one ship every 12 minutes.

They came across the *Nemesis* around 5:30am, lurking up-river, its guns already pitched at one of the forts in anticipation of the peace that had been brokered, failing. Ronan couldn't remember exactly when that was to be, but he knew it would not be long. After all, this was just the first of three Opium Wars.

As with the other vessels, Edmund rowed slowly and gently towards the *Nemesis*, their passage through the water virtually silent. She was an iron-hulled paddle frigate, steam powered, and with a shallow draught, allowing her to travel closer to shore or up-river in pursuit of the smaller Chinese junks where other English ships could not.

Ronan prepared the bombs – connecting the flint, checking the timer, then tying each one back up and painting it with pitch before sticking it to the hull. He tried not to get any of the goop on his hands, but by now they were covered in the awful stuff. He feared it might never wash off.

'Hey! What are you doin' down there? Who are you?!'

They looked up to see a deckhand hanging over the side of the vessel glaring down at them. He raised a lantern to get a better look. 'Who are you?!'

'It's all right, sailor,' Ronan called back as calmly as he could. 'We're just checking for any leaks.'

'This boat doesn't leak.'

Ronan improvised. 'Oh, and you're an expert in … metal boats, are you? Did you design it? Did you build it?! Have you got any idea the kinds of stresses a boat like this has to endure? Ever heard of rust? You want a gigantic rust hole to appear at the bottom of the ship? Or even a whole series of little ones. Imagine all this weight pressing down on a rusted-out bottom. Let's see if she leaks then, shall we? Let's see how long your 'unleakable' boat stays afloat without a hull, shall we?!'

'Why are you doing it at night, then? How can you see anything?'

'You don't look for rust during daylight!' Ronan replied condescendingly 'That would be stupid. By the time you can see it it's already too late. You have to feel for it. You have to smell it. You can't smell anything during the day. Too many other smells around.'

'All right, all right. You're the expert. Get on with it, then,' the sailor ordered, then vanished from the railing; and as the light faded, he could be heard grumbling to himself: 'I knew these iron ships were a bad idea.'

Ronan secured the final bomb to the hull of the *Nemesis*. 'All right. Let's get the hell out of here.'

At 6am sharp the light show began. It spread for miles up and down the Pearl River and was spectacular. Like New Years at sea level. The English forces had been decimated. General Yang was pleased. On his command, as the sun peeked over the horizon, their army of 30,000 soldiers descended on the English positions. Despite their inferior firearms, and with many civilians joining the fray with nothing more than swords and sticks, they pushed the English forces back into the water all along the river.

A key factor in their victory, not to be understated, was the pounding of the drums while Aliyah sang *Seize the Day* from the Disney musical *Newsies*. She had taught the rhythm to their drummers and key parts of the climactic chorus to a choir of Chinese soldiers, and their vigorous chanting of '*One for all and All for One,*' despite the language barrier, actually did inspire the men. It was ridiculous, insane, and yet somehow, it worked.

It even caused the Anomaly to shudder and pulse in sympathy to the rhythm, and its growth was momentarily arrested – though no one noticed this amidst all the chaos.

In just a few hours the tide had turned on the first (and now *only*) Opium War. A comprehensive Chinese victory that would lead to the reclamation of Hong Kong and a new thousand-year dynasty. But despite their success, the Anomaly remained and had by now grown so large it breached the city walls. The future – at least for Chase and Ronan – remained unchanged. Ronan, Edmund and Aliyah reunited and, leaving behind them a changed destiny for the Chinese nation, they leapt into the Doomsday Bubble to see what new fate was in store for them.

CHAPTER 11

Yazata!

Meanwhile, on the field of Marathon on the Greek coast just north of Athens, on September 11 in the year 490 BCE (a Monday according to the modern Gregorian calendar, though of course this was not how things were dated at the time), Chase, Beth and Sergeant Frimmel walked through the camp of the Persian army of the Achaemenid Empire. They were appropriately dressed for the period in holo-uniforms, which were nothing more than quilted jerkins with a cloth or fur Phrygian cap. These would prove woefully inadequate against Athenian spear and armour in the coming battle, which was to be a major turning point in the rise of Greek culture and its influence over all Western civilisation for centuries to come.

The Persian forces numbered 25,000 infantry and 1,000 cavalry, with 600 ships beached or anchored in Marathon Bay. It was one of the largest forces ever assembled in the ancient world. Compare that to a mere 1,000 on the Athenian side, and a Persian victory seemed inevitable.

The field was surrounded by boggy marches that hugged low-lying hills on three sides, and a deep ravine split the field down the middle. The bay flanked the eastern side with the Persian camp to the south of the ravine. On the southern hill the Anomaly could be seen jutting from the mound like a dome, glowing and pulsating as it consumed the hill, and with it, a small temple – the Sanctuary of

Heracles. The shimmering dome overlooked the field like a beacon from the gods sent to witness the coming battle. Many in the camp saw it as an omen – though whether it be good or ill no-one could say. Both sides had sent scouting parties to investigate the giant dome. They never returned. So, when our travellers emerged from the dome and approached the Persian camp, they were believed to be messengers from the gods; and as they passed through the camp, attracting enthralled looks from the soldiers, a path cleared magically before them; and when they asked where they could find the tent of the commander, they were pointed the way without impediment, their guide muttering '*Yazata*' and bowing reverently as they passed.

Frimmel was getting quite expert with his iPhone camera and had learned how to be more discreet in how he held and aimed it. And like any good documentarian, when and when not to film.

Beth had the book open before her as they walked. 'Tomorrow the Greeks will win a decisive victory against the Persians here. If we can ensure the Persians win instead, it will fundamentally alter the future of western civilization. No Plato or Socrates. No theatre or Olympic games. And no democracy.'

'Really?' Chase asked.

'England and the British Empire probably wouldn't even exist if it weren't for the Greeks. And it all comes down to this one battle.'

'What about Germany?' Frimmel asked.

'Probably no Germany either.'

'Maybe this is not such a good idea.' Frimmel said, but the others ignored his protest.

'So how do we make sure the Persians win?' Chase asked.

'I don't know.'

Chase remained confident. 'We'll think of something. After all, it worked out okay with Jesus.'

'Except that it didn't work,' Beth responded. 'The Anomaly is still growing.'

'This time'll be different. Like you said, the whole history of western civilisation is riding on this.'

They arrived at the tent of the Persian commander. A large standard of a yellow eagle against a red background was posted by the entrance, along with two enormous guards – Immortals. These were the elite soldiers of the Persian army who, unlike the regular troops, had scale armour over their tunics and a conical helmet protecting their heads. They carried short spears and shields fashioned of wicker and leather.

'We're here to see General Datis,' Chase proclaimed in perfect pod-translated Persian. 'We bring news of the enemy.' He was their elected spokesperson since Beth, a woman, would not be taken seriously, and as there had not yet been a movie of H.G. Wells *The Time Machine* in the 1930s, Frimmel still didn't quite grasp what was going on.

The guards glanced at the cluster of soldiers gathered behind them – curious to see what happened next – then at the three standing before them.

'Wait here,' one of the immortals said and went inside.

Chase whispered to Beth: 'Did I say that right?' Beth nodded. The remaining guard scowled at them suspiciously. Chase tried not to look intimidated. The first guard returned and motioned for them to enter.

Inside the tent the travellers found a group of men gathered around a table on which were laid maps and plans for the coming battle. At the centre of the group, commanding in both attitude and bearing, stood General Datis, a man in his fifties wearing simple, though colourful, tunic and trousers, and with a shock of curly black hair on his uncovered head. He had the assured manner of a general who was used to winning. At the opposite end of the table stood a much younger man with the same assured manner, though it came from a very different place – the arrogance of youth. This was Artaphernes, nephew to King Darius I, and co-commander of the Persian forces.

'I'm telling you,' Artaphernes proclaimed, 'Athens is undefended. We should put the cavalry back on the ships and send them round the point. They're useless here anyway because of the swampland. Then we can attack the city from land *and* sea.'

Datis appeared uncertain. 'Perhaps.' Then glanced at the three 'soldiers' standing by the entrance.

'What news?'

'According to the Oracle you will lose this battle and the great Persian Empire will fall.' Chase proclaimed, just as Beth had told him.

'Only Athenians believe in the assertions of Oracles,' Datis countered disdainfully. 'We are not so naïve.' Then in a more ominous tone: 'Is that all you came to say?'

'We're here to help,' Chase offered cheerfully, now off-script.

'You can help by fighting when the time comes, soldier,' Artaphernes growled. 'Now leave us.'

'You don't understand. When I said Oracle, I meant... soothsayer... or prophet. You know? Either way, Trust me. You're about to lose, big time.'

'And why should we believe you?' Datis asked pointedly.

Chase tried to come up with a credible lie. 'Because...We are ...'

'– Yazata!' Beth blurted. 'We are Yazata!'

'What are you doing?' Chase asked through grit teeth.

'Yazata means angel,' Beth whispered. 'They think we're angels.'

'No, they're not,' Artaphernes declared contemptuously. 'They're Athenian spies. Arrest them!'

The immortal guards appeared out of nowhere and grabbed the travellers. One of them noticed the silver stick in Chase's hand and took possession of it. Likewise, Frimmel's luger and *camera* were confiscated. Their clothes shimmered and glitched, then disappeared completely, revealing Chase in 2100 suit and tie, Beth in 2018 smart casual dress ensemble, and Frimmel in 1920s German police uniform.

The Persians, astonished by this magic, raised their spears at the group; though some appeared hesitant since their unusual dress suggested these strangers may indeed be Yazata.

Datis stepped forward, sceptical. 'Who are you? Really?'

Beth's understanding of the Zoroastrian faith was scant, so she took a page from Chase's playbook and winged it. 'We come from the gods of Babylon! And we have observed your plans from afar. We know the future, and I tell you now, you will lose this battle unless you do what we say.'

'Gods of Babylon?'

'... And everywhere else.'

Datis stepped up to Beth, looked her up and down. 'You don't look like a god. Or Yazata for that matter. You look like a woman.'

Beth was lost for words. Not just because he was catching her in a lie, but his breath was on her face and her legs became weak all of a sudden. He was an imposing man. 'And you know what Yazata look like, do you?' she challenged.

Datis paused, glancing at the two men standing either side of her in their peculiar clothes. 'You do not look like Athenians.'

'We came from the giant … orb,' Chase declared, inventing yet another name for the Anomaly. 'We have come to help you. But if you don't want our help, we can just as easily go to the Athenians.'

Datis bristled. He motioned for the others to lower their spears, then asked: 'Tell me truthfully, are you sent by Ahura Mazda or Angra Mainyu?'

Beth recalled those names; they were the Zoroastrian equivalent of God and Devil. She remembered which was the good one because he had a car named after him. '...Um ... the first one. Mazda.'

'Ahura Mazda.' Datis repeated. The commanders echoed the name reverently.

Beth nodded. 'Ahura Mazda.'

Datis considered this for a moment, then stepped away and bowed. The other commanders also bowed – though young Artaphernes did so reluctantly. He was still not convinced of their divinity.

'Forgive me,' Datis said. 'What would you have us do?'

Meanwhile, in the year 1204, April 12 (a Monday), Ronan, Edmund and Aliyah found themselves in the middle of a terrifying siege, as the excommunicated soldiers of the Fourth Crusade and their Venetian allies sacked the great city of Constantinople. Our travellers had emerged from the Anomaly in the heart of the metropolis which found itself being consumed from within and assaulted from without. The multi-cultural population of merchants, artisans, nobles and peasants from the East as far as India and China via the silk road, and West as far as the islands that would one day become Great Britain, was made even more diverse by the addition of many travellers from other times who had likewise stumbled into the Anomaly and emerged unprepared into the besieged city.

Panic reigned as the crusaders battered on the city walls with trebuchets and catapults, battering rams and arrows, while contending with plummeting stones, boiling oil and Greek Fire thrown against them by the city's defenders, until finally breaching the walls by cat-walking across from the tall masts of their ships to the top of the towers, or digging through an undefended section and opening the gates from within. By nightfall, people were being indiscriminately slaughtered, and the churches looted for their wealth by men flaunting the cross of the saviour on their uniforms and shields.

Ronan was no expert but he recognised the outfit, with its mail armour, metal helmet, white tunic and red templar cross emblazoned on the chest and shield. When he told Edmund who they were, Edmund was horrified. They were a mere 118 years after Edmund's own time, and the legendary city known as the *Eye of the World* and the capitol of Eastern Christianity was being destroyed by those charged by the Pope with protecting the faith.

Enraged, and despite having no sword or shield of his own, Edmund confronted one of the crusaders as he came out of a church laden with gold and bejewelled treasures and loaded them onto a palfrey. 'What are you doing!' Edmund cried. 'This is sacrilege!'

Edmund pushed at the man, knocking the priceless booty from his hands causing it to tumble and clatter on the ground; these were not just valuable relics, they were works of art. The crusader drew his sword, about to cut Edmund's head from his shoulders. He swung.

Edmund ducked and charged at the crusader, managing to knock him over. The man dropped his sword as his hand hit the pavement. Edmund snatched it up and raised it over his head – but hesitated. He had never killed a man before, let alone a soldier of Christ. Even if he *was* a thief and a murderer.

Ronan and Aliyah could do nothing but stand by and watch, as the crusader got to his feet and indignantly grabbed the blade with his mail armoured hand and snatched it away from Edmund. He raised it again as Edmund froze in a panic. But before he could swing a heavy golden candlestick, thrown by Aliyah, struck the man on the helmet and knocked him off balance.

'Run!' she screamed at Edmund.

Edmund found his feet and fled.

'This way!' a young woman cried who had been watching the confrontation from the shadows. They followed her without question down one of the side streets.

As they fled, Edmund wept. This was all wrong. Everything was wrong. The world didn't make sense anymore. With all that had happened the last few days, the one thing he had clung to was his faith. The infallible teachings of the Church and the vicar of Christ – the Pope. And now that too, was destroyed. What was there left to live for if God permitted such atrocities in his name?

The young woman led our travellers away from the sacking and looting and murder, away from the rapacious destruction and slaughter happening before their eyes in the streets, and away from the Anomaly that was presently consuming parts of the magnificent Hagia Sophia church and the Great Palace. They passed through narrow streets of tall tenements made of stone on the lower floors, and built up several storeys high with wooden extensions. Many of these were already burned to rubble from some previous conflagration.

Indeed, the city appeared more ash and blood than the shimmering crossroads of the world that legend would have.

Eventually they came upon a street where some buildings remained intact.

'In here,' the young woman told them as she made for a nearby house. 'We can hide in here.'

They followed her inside, happy to be off the streets, though they could still hear the battle raging in the distance.

'Thank you,' Ronan said, once the door was closed behind them.

'Yes, thank you,' Aliyah echoed.

The young woman nodded acknowledgement, but her eyes were fixed on Edmund. 'That was very brave of you. Standing up to him like that.'

'It was stupid,' Edmund replied, chastising himself. "I was angry. He would have killed me on the spot if Aliyah hadn't thrown that candlestick. Good pitch, by the way.'

'Thank you,' Aliyah said.

'No. It was admirable,' their young host insisted. 'You were fearless.'

Ronan then realised: 'You speak English.'

'I speak many languages. My people come from York to the north of England. Do you know it?'

Edmund couldn't help but smile. 'I know it well.' Then found himself adding: 'A beautiful place and a noble people.'

'When I heard you speak, I knew you were from the old country,' she told them. 'Plus, your clothes suggest you are travellers and kindred spirits.' They certainly did look different. 'Please come in, sit. You'll be safe here. At least for a while.'

As they walked into the main room of the house, they

discovered a group of people of all shapes and sizes, ages and backgrounds, and all dressed quite colourfully, with hair tied into haphazard bunches, threaded into long plaits, or covered by turbans. Some wore robes with a definite eastern flavour, flowing and loose and decorated with elaborate designs or embroidery, while others took a more 'western' approach to their attire with bold flat colours, stockings and jerkins, tunics and surcoats. Some mixed and matched their fashion so they were a strange amalgam of East (both middle and far) and West (both European and English). They sat around the room on chairs and sofas like an assorted company of bohemian entertainers, all looking curiously at the visitors as they entered, with one old man holding up a thick lens to get a better view of the strangers. By comparison, the newcomers' clothes were quite drab, though unusual. They fit right in.

'What are you doing in Constantinople?' Ronan was in the middle of asking the young woman when they came upon this scene.

'We are troubadours. A travelling circus if you will. We come from all over. My name is Tiffany.'

'I'm Ronan. This is Aliyah, and Edmund.'

'Hello Edmund,' Tiffany said, smiling coyly. She then proceeded to introduce the others in the room, but Edmund wasn't really listening. He was entranced by Tiffany's smile.

'That's an unusual name – Tiffany,' Aliyah ventured, as it sounded odd for the period.

Tiffany thought about it for a moment. 'Not really. We had an empress here by that name not long ago. There's lots of us around. Please, sit. I'll get you some drinks.' Then Tiffany disappeared into the kitchen, as if on a mission.

Ronan leaned in: 'I think she likes you,' he whispered into Edmund's ear.

'What? No. Don't be absurd.'

'And you like her,' Ronan added.

Edmund fumbled for a response, then resorted to brushing his clothes vigorously, wiping away any dust he might have gathered in his fight, while making inarticulate noises of half-hearted protest. What was wrong with him? It's not like he had never had a woman or did not know how to talk to them. He actually considered himself quite good at courting. But the women of his time were timid and reticent, their place in the world clearly defined; and his place as a man, even a lowly one, was nonetheless superior to theirs. He was not used to bold women like Aliyah or Tiffany. He was not used to the fairer sex being quite so brazen.

'Where are you from?' The old man asked.

'England!' Edmund blurted, grateful for the change of subject.

'*Fuck the English,*' Aliyah muttered automatically, even though the joke was now well worn and out of context.

'Ireland,' Ronan said.

'Australia!' Aliyah declared. Then realizing it probably hadn't been discovered yet. 'No wait … America. No...'

'Ethiopia,' Ronan suggested.

Aliyah was about to be offended at the implication, but then saw the logic in it. 'Yeah, that'll do. Ethiopia.'

'It's not important,' another said, allaying any fears he thought our travellers had about their origins. 'We are all *citizens of the world*, as the Greeks would say. Where you are from is not as important as where you are going.'

'Marcus here is the philosopher of our little group,' Matilda teased.

Everyone was being so pleasant; as if nothing at all was

happening in the city beyond their walls.

'And what brings you to Constantinople?' the old man asked.

'Fate,' Ronan said, only half joking. 'Bad luck. Fluctuations in the Higgs field.'

There was a momentary silence as the group tried to comprehend what he was saying. They failed.

'What do you do?' Matilda asked, trying to keep the conversation light.

'I'm a – ' Ronan had to think about it. His degree was in genetic biology, but he'd never pursued it as a career and had forgotten most of it anyway. What he did, more than anything, was sponge off others. His parents. The University. Even Chase. He had come to terms with that, but it's not something he was proud of; and certainly not something he could declare as an occupation. ' – natural philosopher,' he finally said, using the old term for scientist, and once said aloud, felt it approached the truth.

'Ah. That makes sense,' Matilda nodded, since no-one quite understood what he was talking about. 'I'm an acrobat,' she explained. 'So are Friedrich and Yohannes,' indicating the two young men sitting next to her, then pointed across the room. 'Marcus, Stephan and Hildegarde are minstrels,' then gesturing to the old man with the lens, 'Bapoo is a Jester and juggler, and Tiffany is learning the craft from him.'

'I sing and act,' Aliyah told them.

'Excellent! We could use another singer. Perhaps you could grace us with a song.'

Ronan and Edmund groaned – *here it comes*.

'All right, but… are you sure it's safe?' Usually, Aliyah would jump at any invitation to sing, even in the midst of a battle (as she had done at Changzhou). But this was not an army she was singing to; they were circus performers. And they were not on the winning side this time.

'Of course!' Matilda said a little too confidently. 'We could all do with a song right now, yes?' Everyone agreed wholeheartedly.

'All right, then,' Aliyah conceded happily. 'This has been buzzing round my head ever since we got here. You know, like an earworm.'

'A what?'

'An earworm?'

'That sounds disgusting.'

'Anyways.' Aliyah sang: *'Istanbul was Constantinople, now it's Istanbul, not Constantinople....'*

She began to beat out the rhythm on her thighs. The minstrels joined in, with Stephan picking up a small drum and Marcus quickly finding the correct accompanying chords on a lute (there were only two), while Hildegarde picked up the melody on a recorder and joined it. Everyone else soon got into the groove of the fast tempo song and were clapping along.

While this happened, Tiffany returned with beers and sat boldly next to Edmund.

'Your friend is a good singer.'

'Yes. She is.'

Ronan found the beer to have a fruity nose and disproportionately high alcohol content. He liked it, savouring its unusual flavour, while listening in to see how Edmund coped.

'And what do you do, Edmund?' Tiffany asked.

'I...' *What do I do?* Edmund thought. He had been a courtier – a vassal – his entire life. Always at the service of another. His one skill was as a scribe. He kept books and ledgers. That's what he had been trained to do. But it was drudge work, and he certainly didn't consider it a talent. But unable to think of anything else, and not wanting to lie, he said: 'I…write.'

Tiffany was genuinely impressed. 'A writer? That's amazing. I've never met anyone who could write.' Tiffany meant this literally. Writing was a skill few had mastered outside of a monastery; though Constantinople was one city where a scribe could thrive thanks to its rampant bureaucracy and record keeping – all of which was presently being destroyed forever.

'What do you write?'

'Plays,' Edmund lied. 'Stories about kings and tyrants. Faith and treachery. Love and loss.' Because if Edmund were to write a play that's what it would be about.

'You're a poet,' Tiffany told him. Then as Aliyah led the others in a rousing climax to the song – '*Istanbul!*' – Tiffany kissed Edmund full on the mouth. It was an act of desperation, as if they were about to die and this would be her only chance to do so.

Then as the singing stopped, they heard the fire raging outside. The flames warmed the stone and wooden walls of the structure until finally the building was aflame. They were trapped.

CHAPTER 12
Triumphal Quadriga

Meanwhile, in the Persian encampment at Marathon in the year 490 BCE, Chase, Beth and Frimmel had yet to work out how to help the Persians win the battle that was to come.

The big problem with the Persian forces was not their numbers, they outnumbered the Athenians ten to one. It was not their lack of armour. Most of their fighting force were archers who were not meant to fight in close quarters; while the Immortals, who did fight hand to hand, had scaled armour. It was not their cavalry, which was well-trained and, after a few days to recover their land legs, were well fed and rested, while the Athenians had no cavalry at all with them. And it was not the terrain. Despite there being swampland to the south and a ravine to the north which prevented them from deploying the cavalry as they normally would, and despite the Athenians having the higher ground protecting the pass that led through the hills to Athens, the plain of Marathon itself was a perfect place to conduct a battle.

No, the real problem with the Persian forces was that they had two commanders who were in conflict with each other. Datis was the experienced soldier, and if it were left to him their victory over the smaller Athenian force would be assured, just as it had been in every other town throughout the Cyclades up to Eretria – where they had decimated the city and enslaved its people. Athens was next.

Young Artaphernes however, being nephew to Darius the Great, King of Kings, was the 'senior' commander, despite his complete lack of military experience or training. But the king was no fool. Artaphernes was here to learn, which is why he had been teamed with General Datis. And so far, Datis had got his way. But Artaphernes was emboldened by their victories, claiming undue credit for them, and now felt he knew enough to take over. A little knowledge can be a dangerous thing.

'We are not keeping the cavalry here,' Artaphernes said too loudly. 'It's pointless! Much better to send them to Athens on the ships so they can attack from the south.'

'A cavalry,' Datis intoned, 'attacking from the sea.' He had to be careful what he said. This was the King's nephew, after all.

Our newly anointed Yazata's – Chase, Beth and Frimmel – were listening in, as were all the other commanders and various Immortal guards. A feast was being held in their honour because when asked "what would you have us do" Chase didn't have a ready answer. And he was hungry. So he requested a feast. At least it would buy them some time.

Datis was very conscious that everyone in the tent could hear them, but Artaphernes didn't care.

'They won't be attacking from the sea. They'll land first, obviously.'

'So just to be clear,' Datis said calmly. 'The cavalry will land in the bay south of Athens, without meeting any resistance, because all their army is here, after all. Then they'll attack, without archers, somehow scaling the long walls that stretch from the port all the way up to the city, while we, having crushed – that was the word, yes? – crushed the Athenians here, without the use of cavalry, will then march directly on the city and attack from the north.'

135

'It's a good plan,' Artaphernes said, ignoring the barely veiled cynicism in Datis's assessment. 'You just can't handle anyone else taking the lead. Face it, old man. You're out of ideas. You just want to keep doing the same thing over and over again.'

'Because it works.'

'This will work better! My uncle the king gave me command of this army before you. So I outrank you, General. We're doing it.'

'Can I make a suggestion?' Chase ventured. Until now the Yazata had been content to eat the excellent buffet that had been presented to them, listening quietly to the two leaders argue, while they concocted their own plan that would turn things around for the Persians. Beth had now had time to study the details of this famous battle in her book; it seemed the crucial mistake the Persians made was sending the cavalry away, just as Artaphernes was proposing.

All eyes turned to Chase, who was conscious of the political tensions in the room and didn't want to start a civil war. 'While we do appreciate the … unique solution Artaphernes has proposed. We fear this will not work. We agree with General Datis. You need the cavalry here.'

Artaphernes scowled. 'Perhaps your vision of the future is unclear, Yazata. You cannot know – '

'– But we do,' Beth interrupted, rising to her feet. 'We know how this battle will end, and we know why. There is a lot more riding on this that your petty ambitions or even the Persian Empire. That giant orb out there is going to eat everything. Do you understand? It comes from Angra Mainyu and will destroy the world in a few days if you do not win this battle. That is how important this is. Ahura Mazda is watching, and right now he is not happy. You will *not* send your cavalry away. You will put them on the frontline and you will decimate the Greeks. You will take Athens, and you will kill all the men, enslave the women and children and destroy forever any hope of the Greeks becoming an empire in their own right. I want you to wipe them from history! Only then can the giant orb of Angra Mainyu be destroyed, and the world be saved. And I don't care if the king is your uncle you arrogant Persian prick. Sending the cavalry away is a stupid idea. Datis is in charge.'

With that, Beth sat down.

Chase leaned across to Frimmel who was holding up the iPhone. 'Did you get all that?' Frimmel nodded.

The tent had become terrifyingly quiet, until Datis rose to his feet, raised a cup and declared: 'The Yazata have spoken!'

The commanders rose and raised their own cups and drank in solidarity with their true leader – General Datis.

Artaphernes stormed out of the tent. Datis watched him leave and smiled. 'Tomorrow we will crush the Greeks! Destroy their temples! Rape their women! Enslave their children! And the great Persian Empire will rule all the lands to the western sea for a thousand years!!'

The room cheered.

The following morning, at first light, after several days of both sides warily surveying each other across the field, the Persians attacked. Five thousand archers led the way. The two armies were only 1.5 kilometres from each other, so the distance was quickly traversed. Once they were in range (200 metres), the archers loosed a volley of arrows that blotted out the sky. The Athenians were caught off guard. They had seen the Persians coming across the field but were still scrambling to get themselves organised. Another volley was loosed. Then another. Then, as Beth had instructed, the thousand strong cavalry rode through the archers taking the lead, with Immortals and infantry soldiers right behind them. The archers continued firing over their heads until the two armies met. Then it was spear to spear, sword to sword and hand to hand. The Athenians put up a strong defence with their bronze armour, long spears, and phalanx of shields, but it all came too late. The Persians had overwhelmed them, and they had already lost half their force to the archers.

The battle was over in less than an hour. The rocky field of Marathon transformed into a bloodied swamp. Without pausing, Datis led his army through the pass and on to sack Athens which was 40 kilometres south. It would be an 8-hour march but by nightfall, with no army to defend it, the city would be in flames; and the thousand-year rule of the Persian Empire was assured. An empire that was to spread across Europe to the Atlantic Ocean, defeat the invading armies of Alexander the Great, and even thwart the rise of the Roman Empire that was to have been its successor. The country known as England would not be born of Viking, Anglo-Saxon and Roman heritage, but from the migration of Persian and Middle Eastern peoples.

Chase, Beth and Frimmel watched the battle from the southern hill, not far from where the Sanctuary of Heracles had once been – before it had been consumed by the Anomaly. Frimmel turned white with shock at seeing this scene and had to stop filming and sit on the ground before he fainted. Chase and Beth, on the other hand, stood shoulder to shoulder, determined and hopeful that the slaughter on the field below them was worth it. But as they watched Datis lead his army away the Anomaly, rather than vanish, shimmered and grew.

The history of the Greeks was unchanged. Greek culture still flourished even under the thousand-year rule of the Achaemenid Empire. Indeed, many cultures that were otherwise destroyed by centuries of European in-fighting and authoritarian ambitions were to thrive under Persian rule, which turned out to be far more 'democratic' than anything the Greeks or Romans had to offer; and the long tail of history found an equilibrium so that in the end, nothing was changed.

'It didn't work,' Chase said despondently.

'Perhaps the Persians weren't that bad, after all,' was all Beth could say.

'Why did you bring me here?' Frimmel asked from the ground. 'Why did you make me witness that? You're both monsters!'

'If that's what it takes,' Chase said dispassionately.

'We're all monsters when it comes down to it,' Beth told Frimmel tenderly, as a mother might comfort her child before the bombs drop. 'Just civilised monsters.'

'I want to go home,' Frimmel whimpered.

'Too late for that,' Chase told him. 'Like it or not, you're along for the ride.'

'I want to go home,' Frimmel just repeated.

A silence fell between them for several seconds, each of them lost in their thoughts. Until finally:

'Maybe we're going about this all wrong,' Beth suggested.

'How do you mean?' Chase asked.

'We keep trying to fix things. Maybe we should break something.'

'We just broke the history of Greek civilisation and nothing changed. It's like humans are destined to crawl out of the swamp and evolve to take over the world, and Ronan and me are destined to create this thing and destroy it all.'

Frimmel got to his feet. 'I refuse to take part in this anymore. I'm going home.'

'Why?' Chase said. 'It'll all be gone in a couple of days anyway.'

Incensed, Frimmel snatched the Pod from Chase's hand and ran into the Anomaly.

'Hey! Give that back!'

'Hans!' Beth yelled after him.

Chase and Beth clasped hands and as one, dived into the Anomaly after him.

Meanwhile in Constantinople – formerly called Byzantium and later to be known as Istanbul – the house that had been the refuge of the travelling players had been set aflame by the Crusaders of the Holy Roman Empire; a crusade initiated by Pope Innocent III to liberate Jerusalem from the Muslim heretics, and which was now hell-bent on the murder, rape, destruction, and plunder of Rome's sister city.

Tiffany and her troupe of performers, along with Ronan, Aliyah and Edmund, ran to the rear of the house and out into the communal courtyard. All the buildings around the courtyard were in flames. The upper wooden floors were raging while the lower stone sections of the buildings were beginning to crumble under the inferno.

'This way!' Marcus called, and he led them all into a passage between two of the buildings, which, despite the fire raging in the arch overhead, offered a path out to the street. Hot embers fell from above as beams turned to charcoaled ash and began to crumble. The last of them, old Bapoo the jester, helped by Tiffany and Edmund, made it out just as the beams collapsed behind them and the entire archway and several floors above tumbled into the alley, now blocking the exit.

They found themselves on a narrow street, where every building that had not already been burned to a crisp by earlier fires was now in flames. They ran up the street, away from the flames and back towards the Hagia Sophia church and the Anomaly – from the fire to the frying pan.

The invaders – Crusaders in their holy regalia and Venetians in their humbler armour – were too busy looting to notice our party of travellers. Anyone who got in their way – man or child – was quickly dispatched; and any woman foolish enough to still be about was taken aside and violated. But if you stayed out of their way and kept to the shadows, they ignored you. Their eyes saw only gold and jewels.

Our travellers watched as a group of Venetians carried four full-sized bronze horses through the streets on a cart; or rather, the bodies of the bronze steeds. Their severed bronze heads rolled about in the cart at their feet. These were the Triumphal Quadriga, removed from the gates of the Hippodrome and destined for Venice where they would live out the rest of their lives on the terrace of Saint Mark's Basilica (notwithstanding a brief interruption by Napoleon Bonaparte who was to steal them for himself).

They also witnessed a man with a prominent monobrow and dressed in fine clothes dashing towards the docks with two women, likewise dressed in expensive tailored silks with flowing sleeves. 'That's the Emperor Mourtzouphlos,' Bapoo told them, holding up his lens to get a better look. 'Yep. Definitely him. We performed for him just last week.'

The reign of Mourtzouphlos (officially Emperor Alexios V)

had lasted just two months, and now that his city was in flames he was running away.

'Typical,' Bapoo spat.

Ronan spotted the crest of the Anomaly pulsating in the distance. 'Come on,' he called and took the lead. As they reached the Hagia Sophia, Crusaders were desperately trying to 'save' the treasures from within the church before the growing Anomaly devoured them. Meanwhile a swarm of refugees were leaping into the sphere to escape the city – whatever lay on the other side of this giant orb must surely be better than staying to die in Constantinople.

'Everyone hold hands!' Ronan told them as they joined the throng of refugees. 'It gets a bit rough in there!' Ronan grabbed Aliyah, who grabbed Edmund, who grabbed Tiffany, who grabbed Bapoo, and on down the line until they were all connected and moved into the Anomaly as one long chain of human desperation. Once Ronan had entered the others were hauled into the vortex with increasing velocity, lifting those at the back of the line clear off their feet as they were pulled in. Other citizens, hearing Ronan's instruction, followed suit and held the hands of their loved ones before they leapt into the unknown.

In the days to come the looting of Constantinople would continue, making it the largest and most destructive robbery in all of history; but thanks to the Anomaly, which had consumed several churches, the Great Palace, and most significantly the great library of Constantinople, these were spared the sacking they would otherwise have endured, and were preserved (after a fashion) within the vortex, possibly to be spat back out at some other time and place; as were the many refugees from the city, and the people and creatures from countless other times who had blundered, marched, or willingly succumbed to the Giant Orb/Hellgate/Doomsday Bubble/Anomaly that Chase and Ronan had created, and which was now just days away from consuming the entire universe.

CHAPTER 13
Deus Ex Machina

Frimmel had run off with the Pod in hopes of finding his way home, but had no idea how to use the device. Upon falling into the Hellgate his body was violently whipped about the maelstrom, but he remained focused on the Pod, ignoring the millennia of history tumbling about him as he randomly pushed its buttons.

Something grabbed his foot. Frimmel looked down to find Chase attached to his leg. 'Give it back Frimmel. You don't know what you're doing!'

Beth had hold of Chase's other hand. 'We'll take you home, Hans. I promise!'

'No, you won't!' Frimmel yelled back over the sound of a whale colliding with the dome of the Taj Mahal. Frimmel continued pushing buttons, trying to recall what he had seen Chase do. The virtual screen suddenly appeared – *hurrah!* – though he had no grasp of what it displayed or how to navigate it.

'Please, Hans!' Chase begged.

Somehow Frimmel pressed a combination that set new coordinates for the Pod and by pressing the big red button on the device – as he had seen Chase do – the new destination was engaged. The Pod instantly pulled them towards the event horizon of the bubble.

'Where are we going? Beth yelled.

'I have no idea,' Chase yelled back.

Frimmel, Chase and Beth emerged from the Hellgate onto a lush plain covered in long grass. In the near distance was a snow-capped mountain range with a dense forest cascading across the foothills right up to the edge of the plain. There was absolutely no sign of human habitation.

A large herd of elephants grazed nearby.

… No …

…mammoths. They appeared unconcerned by the giant glowing dome dominating the otherwise uniform plain, or indeed by the three humans that had just appeared out of it. A few of the creatures looked at them, saw no threat, snorted, and returned to eating the grass. Feeling too close to a group of large (even if, for the moment, peaceful) animals, our travellers made for the forest.

'Where are we?' Frimmel asked. 'This isn't Munich.'

'Give me the Pod,' Chase demanded.

'No,' Frimmel told him. 'I think I will hold on to it for now.'

'You don't know how to use it.'

'As long as I have it, I am in charge. You will listen to me.'

Chase tried to snatch it away from him, 'Just give it back you stupid Nazi.'

Frimmel pulled out his luger and aimed it at Chase. 'I am not a Nazi! I was fighting the Nazis when you dragged me into that thing. I am a policeman. And you are still under arrest!'

'Hans,' Beth said quietly. 'Please. Put the gun away. You don't really want to hurt us, do you?'

'No. Just him. He always makes fun of me. Thinks I am stupid because I like the movies, or because I am young. You are not much older than me, but you look down on me.'

'I do not!' Chase argued.

'Yes, you do,' Beth countered.

'What?'

'You do it with everyone. At first, I thought it was just because you're English. That's what I liked about you. You're frank – a real hot-dog. But you can be a bit of a wiener sometimes.'

'I agree with this,' Frimmel nodded. 'You are a real wiener würstchen.'

'A what?'

'A Frankfurter.'

'Hey,' Chase was at a loss. 'I'm just trying to save the universe.'

'Fine,' Beth said. 'But you don't have to be a prick about it.'

'I want an apology,' Frimmel said as he waved the gun in Chase's face.

'What for?'

'For being a prick. And for calling me a Nazi.'

'He is definitely not a Nazi,' Beth agreed.

'Okay. I'm sorry I called you a Nazi.'

'…And?'

'And for being a prick,' Chase mumbled, but it sounded genuine.

'Say 'I am a Wiener Würstchen.''

Chase was confused. 'You are a – '

'No. *You* are a Wiener Würstchen.'

Chase sighed 'I am a Wiener Würstchen.'

Frimmel smiled.

'Can you please put the gun away?' Beth asked.

Frimmel returned the gun to its holster.

'Can I have the Pod back now?' Chase asked meekly.

'Who's in charge?' Frimmel said, his hand still on the holster.

'You are.'

Frimmel handed the Pod over.

'Thank you.'

'So Wiener,' Frimmel addressed Chase by his new nickname, 'where are we?'

Chase called up the screen and checked the coordinates. 'We're in the year 305,128 BCE, somewhere in the Middle East.'

'How did we get here?'

Chase glared at Frimmel but said nothing. He enabled the bio-security on the Pod – something he should have done sooner but just forgot.

'How far back does that thing go?' Beth asked, indicating the Anomaly behind them.

'To the beginning of time,' Chase said dryly. 'That's what I've been trying to tell you. All of time will be erased if we don't stop it.'

They reached the edge of the forest and sat down against the trees.

'So what now?' Beth asked as she pulled out a blade of grass and started to pensively wrap it around her fingers.

'I don't know.' Chase was out of ideas. 'No matter what we try everything just goes back to the way it was – or will be. Which means everything ends in about two days. He turned to Frimmel. 'What do you think we should do?'

'Me?'

'You're in charge now.'

Frimmel panicked. 'I think we should go home.'

'There's no going back,' Chase told him.

Frimmel started to cry.

'Hans?'

'I never said goodbye to Ilsa.'

'Ilsa?' Beth was mortified. 'Who is Ilsa?'

'She is my girlfriend.'

'I didn't know.'

Frimmel wiped his face. 'You didn't ask.'

Then they heard movement in the bushes, and they froze.

'Something's there,' Beth whispered.

'Get out your gun, Hans,' Chase ordered.

Frimmel obeyed.

Chase clicked his tongue, hoping to draw out whatever it was, hoping it was nothing more than a rabbit or a fawn or some other harmless, small prehistoric creature. He clicked again.

Eventually something did emerge… a human.

…No…

… A hominid. It was a male – a man – holding out a stone-tipped spear as he walked into the light. He wore animal skin clothes, had long black hair and a round face with a prominent brow. Neanderthal.

He was not alone. More Neanderthals emerged from behind the trees. It was a hunting party of a dozen or so men and within seconds our travellers were surrounded by stone-age spears.

'Put the gun away, Hans,' Chase said calmly, raising his hands in surrender. The others followed suit.

One of the hunters stepped closer. Sniffed. He turned and said something to the others. They laughed a little.

'They talk.' Chase was genuinely surprised.

'Neanderthals were not as dumb some people think,' Beth explained.

Equally surprised, the lead hunter said something that might have been '*They talk!*' in his language. He had never heard a 'human' speak so articulately before.

Chase looked at the Pod, 'The translator's not working.'

'It can't speak Neanderthal,' Beth reasoned.

'What do they want?' Frimmel asked anxiously. 'Are they cannibals?'

Chase might have argued both the logic and semantics of that statement, but now was not the time. (Little did he know that Frimmel was not far from the truth.)

The Neanderthal leader said something, and the hunters lowered their spears. He stepped up to Chase and looked the young Englishman in the eye. Chase returned the gaze, trying not to appear intimidated. Despite the man's gruff appearance, stout frame and clear physical superiority, his eyes were gentle, intelligent, and shrewd. He came to a decision, then placed a heavy hand on Chase's shoulder – a gesture of friendship. Chase returned the gesture, his right hand rested upon the man's left shoulder. Chase was taller, but he still felt as if he were looking up at the Neanderthal man. It occurred to him how astonishing this scene was, and how, if circumstances were different, the Anomaly could be a boon to archaeologists and historical researchers. He was half inclined to ask Frimmel to film the moment, but the Neanderthals might see this action as a threatening gesture, so he let it be for now.

The Neanderthal leader grunted something and gestured for them to follow.

'You can be in charge,' Frimmel said quietly as they moved deeper into the forest. Beth took the young policeman's hand and squeezed it reassuringly. She was just as scared as he was.

After a half hour's walk, they came upon a cave with a wide mouth, set into the side of a prominent, though not overly large, hillside. By this point Frimmel had, in fact, pulled out Beth's iPhone and was filming their journey. 'They're actually cavemen,' Frimmel said. 'Just like in the *Three Ages*.' Chase and Beth didn't get Frimmel's reference to the Buster Keaton movie. 'I wonder if they ride around on dinosaurs like in the movie?'

Outside the cave, as it was a pleasant day, women were working – weaving strands of dried elephant grass into mats or baskets, or cracking seeds and stripping root vegetables for food; while children played nearby, chasing each other around or climbing trees as children of all generations are wont to do. They paused in their labours and games when the strangely dressed (and strangely *human*) visitors entered the space.

The visitors were led inside the cave. It was a bit gloomy, though sunlight spilled in from outside. The cave was separated into different sections. There were no walls or rooms, but there was definitely a 'kitchen' area with a water receptacle, slabs of freshly slaughtered meat and a preparation 'table', a sleeping area with animal fur blankets, and a dining area with large stones set about as seats. The human guests were offered a 'seat' and some food – mashed vegetable with strips of cooked meat in a shallow bowl and with a wooden 'spoon'.

'What exactly is this?' Frimmel asked, inspecting the meat.

'Probably one of those mammoths we saw earlier,' Beth reassured, given the slabs of meat on display were quite large.

Frimmel was not convinced and stuck to the mash.

A large campfire dominated the centre of the cave, surrounded by stones to keep the embers in, the smoke gathering in a convex dome in the ceiling and travelling out through a hole that had clearly been 'drilled' for the purpose. These were no primitive cavemen. They had tools, they had fire, they cooked. They wore clothes that were tanned, stitched, and 'tailored'. The children had toys after a fashion. The women wore jewellery made of bone and ivory, quartz and aquamarine. They had social order that, at least within this small group, seemed to work remarkably well. And they were welcoming and charitable. For the period, these Neanderthals were far more civilised than the hominid ancestors of Chase, Beth and Frimmel.

'You know,' Beth said, 'we all have a little bit of Neanderthal in us. What if it was more than a little bit?'

Chase was intrigued. 'Go on.'

'What if homo sapiens never evolve, and Neanderthals become the dominant species.'

'But then we'd be effectively doing the same thing as the Anomaly,' Chase argued dispassionately, as if it was a purely academic question. 'Destroy all human civilisation before it even had a chance.'

'But the planet would survive. The universe would survive. And who knows, maybe Neanderthals would do a better job as the alpha species. They couldn't do any worse than us homo sapiens.'

'We are all cavemen at heart,' Frimmel muttered, chewing on his mash while a group of Neanderthal children watched them curiously. He picked up the iPhone and filmed the kids. They ran away, giggling.

'Why did they die out?' Chase asked Beth. 'What made homo sapiens so superior? I mean look at them. They cook and have spoons! And they're bigger than us. What makes us so special?'

'Nothing,' Beth said. 'We're not stronger. Or smarter. We're just more violent. We kill anything that stands in our way. The Neanderthals were probably too peaceful for their own good.'

'Then we should teach them how to fight back,' Chase suggested excitedly. 'How to defend themselves.'

'You mean how to wage war.'

'If history's taught us anything it's that humans are violent and stupid and don't deserve to live.'

'So you want to make them like *us*?' Beth challenged.

'Not like us. Better than us.'

'So they can commit genocide even more efficiently than humans.'

Chase paused. 'That's not what I meant.'

'Yes, it is.'

They fell silent.

Finally, Chase muttered: 'You're right. It was a bad idea.'

'You'll think of something,' Beth said, her tone softening immediately. She genuinely admired Chase and was confident he *would* think of something. Or was that confidence misplaced because she was falling in love with him?

Frimmel, who had succumbed to his hunger and was now eating the meat, spoke up. 'I think you are wrong. We are not all violent and stupid. There are good people in this world, and they will always win out in the end.'

'This isn't one of your movies, Hans,' Beth said. 'We don't always get a happy ending.'

Frimmel paused eating, genuinely affronted. 'How can you say that? What has happened to you both that you are so pessimistic?'

'Wait and see what becomes of your precious Fatherland in a few years,' Beth intoned ominously.

'What?!'

'Most of us are capable of monstrous things given half a chance, despite good people like yourself.' Beth was thinking about World War Two; about the stupid, violent history of humanity; and about how she had killed a man in cold blood because she believed he was a monster. How was she any different?

'All I wanted was to go to a party and meet Stephen Hawking,' Chase said out loud.

'You didn't know this would happen,' Beth said. 'It was an accident.'

Chase shook his head. 'There are no accidents. Ronan and I were destined to create this anomaly and destroy the universe, and it seems nothing we do can change that. All of human history has been fated from the start, with me as its final act of hubris.' Chase put his head in his hands – defeated.

Frimmel was incensed. 'Is that it? You give up? So you give us a *Deus Ex Machina* to solve the world's problems – by *destroying* it?! – instead of trying to solve them for ourselves. What is wrong you both? You're such cowards! Of course we fight. And we fight for what is right and good and noble.' He turned on Beth. 'I don't know what you mean by what will become of my fatherland, but if it is bad, I will fight it, as my father did in the Great War. He died to protect me and my mother. To protect our home.' Frimmel rose to his feet. 'That's why I became a policeman. To fight for what was right. A society needs both order and free will. This is what *Metropolis* teaches us. This is what all great drama teaches us. You need order, but you also need a little chaos. It is the stone in the shoe. The grit that forms the pearl. It is imagination honed by adversity. It is at the very heart of what makes us human!' He gestured to the Neanderthals, who were now moving away from this loud young German and regretting having invited them inside.

'And that is why these people will fail,' Frimmel declared. 'They have imagination but no adversity. No grit. They are content! And therefore, they are doomed. If not by us then by some other more ambitious species. You see, I *do* understand where we are and what is going on. Do not take me for a fool. And I believe in happy endings, and not in *Deus Ex Machina*s. But you have to work for it. You have to fight for it. Otherwise, what is the point? What is the point of any of it?!'

Frimmel had run out of steam and sat back down. The cave was now empty, his impassioned speech having scared away their hosts. The Neanderthal leader and a group of hunters appeared at the cave entrance – spears at the ready.

'I think it's time we left,' Chase said.

After thanking them for the food, and receiving a cold stare in return, they were escorted away from the cave, back to the edge of the forest, with a stern warning never to return. They didn't understand the words – but they got the meaning.

Back on the plain, the mammoths had moved on and the land was deserted – except for the Anomaly glowering in the distance. But the long walk back had given Chase time to think.

'You know, Hans, you're absolutely right. Only it's not order and chaos, it's Relativity and Quantum Mechanics. We've been trying to disrupt the timeline to change the outcome, but we're doing it at the wrong level. We need to do it at a quantum level somehow. Revive uncertainty.'

'Okay,' Beth said, not really understanding. 'How do we do that?'

'I don't know. I wish Ronan was here. Somehow, he always manages to hit upon the right solution without even trying. He has an instinct for it.'

'So, let's go find Ronan and the others.'

'How? They could be anywhere?'

'Then... let's go anywhere.'

'And then home?' Frimmel asked hopefully.

'Yes, Hans,' Chase said confidently. 'One way or another, we'll get you back home to Ilsa.'

Meanwhile, in Weimar, Germany, in the year 1716, Johann Sebastian Bach sat at the keyboard of the newly installed and rather enormous pipe organ of St. Paul's Cathedral, while an equally enormous choir of male, female and child singers filled the chancel at the front of the Cathedral.

As Ronan, Aliyah and Edmund tumbled out of the Anomaly, the ominous opening chords of Bach's famous Toccata and Fugue in D minor assaulted their ears. Following Edmund came Tiffany, Bapoo, and the other members of the troupe, all refugees from Constantinople and the terrifying Fourth Crusade of Pope Innocent III, all holding hands and still together after being flung about the vortex within the Giant Orb.

The sublime spectacle of St Paul's cavernous interior, the massive organ pipes, and the beautifully robed choir, was marred by the monstrous Anomaly which had taken a bite out of the north wall of the structure and threatened to consume the whole church. Despite this, a fearful crowd had gathered in the Cathedral, seeking sanctuary and solace from the terrifying bubble, as if the music of Bach would somehow render it harmless, or cast it back to the devil from whom it had obviously come.

'Where are we?' Tiffany asked, astonished.

'When are we?' Aliyah added.

They could barely hear each other over the music. The organ was, after all, the loudest instrument on the planet at the time and this was one of the loudest works ever composed for it, with block chords that rattled the stained-glass windows high above them. And it was having an effect. The Anomaly was awash with colour and patterns, swirling in sympathy to the music.

Aliyah leaned in so Ronan could hear her – it was like trying to hold a conversation at a rock concert. 'Look at the bubble! I saw this happen back in New York!'

'It responds to music,' Ronan said.

'I have seen this too,' Edmund added. 'On the great ship when the band played.'

'Can we use that?' Aliyah asked Ronan.

The Toccata ended and transitioned into the opening bars of a piece that would come to be known by English speakers as *Jesu, Joy of Man's Desiring*.

… And then the choir began to sing.

Edmund was overwhelmed and fell to his knees. He had never heard such music before. Tiffany, equally enthralled, knelt beside him, as if they were praying; as if in that moment they were being wed before God and the celestial music of J.S. Bach.

Then they noticed the Anomaly begin to shrink. It swirled and pulsed and withdrew from the Cathedral as if the prayers of the congregation and the voices of the heavenly choir were indeed compelling the Doomsday Bubble all the way back to Hell from whence it came.

'It's shrinking. But why?' Ronan mused aloud. 'Why music? It's just ... sound, after all.'

'It is more than sound,' Edmund said. 'It is the music of God.'

'Perhaps it is the music of the spheres?' suggested Bapoo.

'The what?'

'According to Pythagoras, all the universe is guided by a mathematical harmony,' Bapoo explained. 'The music of the spheres.'

'Yes!' Edmund agreed. 'Aristotle teaches this also!'

Ronan was confused. 'Pythagoras. He's the maths guy, right? Angles and shit.'

Aliyah punched Ronan –

'*Ow!*'

– She gestured to their surroundings. 'Language.' It may not have been a theatre, but there was still a performance happening.

Edmund became philosophical. 'It is the divine order which controls all the universe and gives harmony to chaos.'

Tiffany, her passions aroused by the music and who had always had a thing for intellectual men, pounced on Edmund in a fervent embrace. Edmund did not object.

'But that's not how the universe works,' Ronan complained.

'Why? Because Einstein said so? Maybe he was wrong.'

'You don't understand, Aliyah.'

'What's to understand? It's working. That's all that matters.'

Ronan nodded. She was right. 'We have to find the others. We have to tell Chase about this. He'll know what to do.'

Ronan and Aliyah headed back to the shrinking Anomaly. Aliyah paused. 'Edmund. Come on!'

Edmund was too preoccupied with Tiffany to hear.

'Stop making out, you randy medieval peasant!'

Edmund came up for air. 'But the music is so beautiful.'

'I'll get you the CD. You gotta help us save the universe, man.'

'I'm not going without Tiffany!'

'And I'm not going without the others,' Tiffany insisted.

'Whatever. Let's go!'

They all clasped hands again. 'How are we gonna find them?' Aliyah asked Ronan as they approached the Bubble.

'I have no idea!'

CHAPTER 14

Rampaging Monkey

The chain of Ronan–Aliyah–Edmund–Tiffany–Bapoo–Matilda–Friedrich–Yohannes–Marcus–Stephan–Hildegarde was flung about the inner vortex of the Anomaly, letting fate and fortune decide where they went and how they landed. The space was filled with refugee travellers from other times. Most were confused, alarmed or just freaking out; some were awed and bewildered; and a few even appeared to be enjoying themselves, having escaped whatever terrible circumstance had been their life moments before.

Because our travellers were a long chain of people from different times, each with their own destinies, dreams and desires, they were independently pulled in different directions by the time eddies, as if it was trying to eject them to a time and place best suited to their individual fates. But the chain held tight, so as the group was pulled one way by one person, another in the chain pulled them in a different direction. In this way they cartwheeled and lurched about the vortex, an eleven-body problem of haphazard symmetry. Eventually those on the ends – Ronan and Hildegarde – were able to join hands and they became a circle. Pulling themselves in, they were able to bundle up into a tight ball of human flotsam. Eleven people, desperately clinging together, their fates now bound to one another.

'This is cosy,' Bapoo said without irony.

'So what do we do now?' Aliyah asked Ronan.

'Just go with the flow, I guess. And keep an eye out for the others.'

They spun around the vortex like this for … well, time was irrelevant, but it seemed like forever. Occasionally they would bump into other time travelling debris – sometimes another living creature, sometimes human, but usually it was something inanimate like a building, boulder, armoire, or tree. They all managed to turn about facing outward, arms locked at the elbow, allowing them to rebuff any object by pushing it away with their feet. This went on for some time and they made a kind of game out of it, seeing how many of them could bounce the group off any object at one time, and how big a push they could muster. Until –

'I see them!' Aliyah declared. 'Ten o'clock!'

Ronan looked up and saw Chase and Beth – hands clasped – and that German policeman who had caused them to separate in the first place was still with them.

'Chase!' Ronan called.

'Beth!' Aliyah called.

Chase and Beth heard their names and turned to the sound.

'Ronan! | Aliyah!'

The two groups tried to 'swim' their way toward one another, but there was no tide to push against. An odd-looking eight-wheeled car floated past Chase (a Reeves-Overland Octoauto from 1911, to be specific). He pushed off this, launching them in the right direction towards the others.

Meanwhile Ronan spotted a passing soldier from the American Civil War with an abundant moustache, long curly locks, and dressed in yankee blues. He had one hand clinging tightly to the reins of his horse, while the other hand was planted on his head to ensure his hat didn't fly away. The poor animal was trying to swim as if it were in water, while its lanky rider floated above it like a lumbering gazelle. Ronan reached out and snatched the rope hanging from his saddle. The soldier objected, but he and his horse were already drifting away as they were pulled towards an exit where he could be heard crying *'What in tarnation is this horseshit!'* before crossing the horizon to emerge in 260 BCE India, the time of the Kalinga War of Ashoka, one of the bloodiest in history, and the lesson of what a true Indian massacre was like.

'Chase! Grab the rope!' Ronan called as he flung the rope across the weightless void. Both Chase and Frimmel reached for the line with their free hands, but the vortex pulled them away.

Ronan retrieved the rope and tried again, as each group pushed themselves off passing debris in an effort to get closer. This went on for some time, with several near misses. Finally, with the rope just inches away, a monkey floated by and desperately grabbed hold of the line.

'Use the monkey!' Beth cried.

Chase stretched and managed to grab the monkey's tail. The monkey turned and hissed as Chase pulled it towards him.

Frimmel was able to grab the rope. 'Got it!'

Chase let go the monkey's tail, but now the monkey was pissed. It lashed out at its new enemy. Frimmel shook the rope trying to throw the monkey off, but this just pissed it off even more. Howling furiously the monkey flung itself onto Chase and climbed up his arm onto his back.

Chase screamed!

He reached around with his free hand, snatching at furry limbs but unable to get a grip. Beth, both hands otherwise occupied, could only look on in horror as the monkey began beating Chase around the head and scratching at his face.

'AH! Fuck! Get this thing off me!'

Chase tried to shake the creature, clutching at it desperately while keeping his grip on Beth, and while still being tossed about by the vortex.

Frimmel pulled the rope in. 'Beth, take the rope.' She let go his right hand and grabbed the line. Frimmel tied the end around her waist. With one hand now free, Beth reached over her head, grabbed the monkey by the scruff of its neck, and tore it away from Chase, hurling the squealing animal away into the vortex. She pulled Chase close into an embrace. His face looked like a Wes Craven movie.

'Was that a Macaque?!' Ronan called from the other end of the line.

'Yeah!' Chase moaned.

'Told you, didn't I! Fuckin' Macaques!'

Now that they were tethered Ronan wrapped the rope around his arm. Then his group finally caught a rip and were pulled upward and out. Chase, Beth and Frimmel were pulled up and out with them

–

– Ronan's group, bound together in a tight cuddling ball of humanity, were spat out of the Anomaly and onto a grassy parkland area on the outskirts of what was once Cambridge University in the year 2100. It was night.

Seconds later Chase, Beth and Frimmel emerged still tethered. Ronan and Aliyah ran to Chase and Beth and embraced the hugging pair. Aliyah cried. Beth cried. Even Ronan cried. Chase was already crying due to the trauma of his monkey scars.

'Jeeze, that macaque really had a go at you,' Ronan said, now that he saw Chase up close.

Beth gently touched Chase's face. 'They'll heal,' she reassured.

Chase looked at Edmund and the others standing with him. He waved, Edmund waved back. 'You seem to have gathered quite an entourage.'

'What the hell are you doing back here!?'

The lads turned to see Professor Alice Beauchamp sitting in a lawn chair, surrounded by the rest of the university faculty, likewise sitting in lawn chairs. Some had shotguns trained on our travellers, ready to shoot anything that emerged from the Anomaly which might be a threat.

In one voice Ronan and Chase declared: 'Professor Beauchamp!'

'Lower your weapons, boys,' Alice told the faculty; then, looking at Chase, 'What happened to you?'

'Rampaging monkey.'

Alice didn't care. 'And who are these people? I didn't send you back so you could fraternize with the natives.'

'We're a team!' Aliyah pronounced.

'Oh, really.'

'Yeah,' Ronan admitted. 'They've been helping us.' He pointed at Frimmel. 'Although I have no idea about this one. He just kind of tagged along.'

'This is Hans,' Chase said. 'He's cool.'

Frimmel smiled. He was part of a team.

Alice shook her head. 'Well, it's not working. Why haven't you erased yourselves from history yet?'

'We can't,' Chase told her. 'Nothing we do makes any difference. But I have a new theory. It involves gravity waves and aetherium energy. If we can just work out how to execute it.'

'We got this,' Ronan said.

'Huh?'

'Tell them, Aliyah.'

'Me?'

'It was your idea,'

'It was Bapoo and Edmund who came up with it.'

'That's okay,' Bapoo gestured. 'You tell it.'

'Will someone just say it?' Alice was getting annoyed.

'It is the music of the spheres,' Edmund said. 'It has been shown to suppress the Doomsday Bubble.'

'The what?'

'I call it a Hellgate,' Frimmel added.

'The Anomaly,' Ronan explained. 'Music. It goes all mushy and shrinks when you play music at it. The louder the better.'

Chase was intrigued. 'How do you know this?'

'We saw it,' Aliyah answered. 'You should have seen it when Bach played the organ at it.'

'You met Bach?' Beth asked.

'Didn't get time to chat,' Aliyah told her.

'And from what I can tell,' Ronan continued, 'it responds best to the human voice. Really makes it cringe.'

Chase was lost. 'How is that possible? We tried everything.'

'We didn't sing at it,' Ronan said.

'Sound waves,' Chase thought aloud. 'But that would mean music is a fundamental property of the universe.'

'Music of the spheres,' Edmund muttered in agreeance.

'A previously unknown field that serves as a kind of spacetime glue. And we interfered with that. Made it inconsonant somehow. Playing music induces a structured wave of harmonic quantum probability in this field. Resets the imbalance. Brings things back into phase.'

Ronan leaned in to Aliyah. 'Told you he'd get it.'

'And you say it shrinks?'

'Yep. Goes all psychedelic and – ' Ronan held up an invisible shrinking ball and crushed it into a singularity, adding appropriate sound effects.

'Prove it,' Alice said.

Chase and Ronan hesitated as they tried to think of a quick experiment that would show what they meant. Then Aliyah sang, belting out the final chorus to *Defying Gravity* from *Wicked*. The Anomaly responded with a kaleidoscope of colour, swirling and churning in the spot where Aliyah's voice was impacting it.

'There!' Ronan declared. 'See! But it needs to be bigger. Louder.'

'Are you thinking what I'm thinking?' Chase asked.

'I think I'm thinking what you're thinking,' Ronan replied, 'if you're thinking what I'm thinking.'

'I think so.'

They turned to Alice. 'Professor?'

'Do what you gotta do, lads. Just hurry up about it before this thing reaches London.'

Chase turned to the others. 'We need musicians.'

Marcus, Stephan and Hildegarde stepped forward. 'Right here.'

'And singers. Lots of singers.'

Aliyah smiled. 'I can help with that.'

CHAPTER 15
Welcome to Rikers Island

Our now rather large group of travellers (fourteen in all) were all tethered together by rope they had sourced rather cheaply from a nearby Cambridge hardware store that was having an *End of the Universe* sale. Thus tied, they emerged from the Anomaly in New York City in the year 2018 – home for Aliyah and Beth. By now all of mid-town Manhattan as far north as Harlem had been consumed by the Bubble, so they emerged onto West 125th not far from the Apollo Theater. Aside from the missing parts that had been swallowed up by the Doomsday Bubble, and the random time travellers wandering the streets, the city looked much as it always had; and though largely deserted, a few native New Yorkers continued to go about their business as if nothing were wrong (like those in the 60s, they weren't about to let a little thing like The End of the World stop them from pursuing their dreams).

Chase, face now covered in antiseptic lotion and tiny band-aids, was at the head of the chain holding onto the Pod, which had accurately guided them to the appointed time and place. However, as they emerged, they were again confronted by a barricade of army and police in tanks and armored vehicles, with all lights and weapons trained on our travellers.

'Not again,' Chase moaned.

Moments later they were all bundled into the back of an army transport, along with several other travellers from different eras.

'At least we're not handcuffed this time,' Ronan said.

'What do we do now?' Edmund asked.

'We escape,' Aliyah said. 'Like last time.'

Chase shook his head despondently. 'Can't. They took the Pod.'

Ronan scowled. 'Why didn't you hide it like before?'

Chase shot Ronan a dirty look before Beth intervened. 'We have to explain to them we know how to stop it.'

'They won't believe us.'

'Ich habe keine Ahnung, was Sie alle sagen,' Frimmel said quietly, 'aber ich stimme zu.' The Pod translator was out of range. Beth placed a hand on Frimmel's shoulder. She didn't understand the words, but the sentiment was clear.

'Perhaps, all of us together, can subdue our captors,' Edmund suggested, 'when they remove us from this carriage.'

Ronan laughed a little. 'Even if we could, we'll still be inside a heavily guarded military base.'

'That's not where they're taking us,' Aliyah said. She could tell by turns of the vehicle.

She was right. They were being taken to Rikers Island.

Rikers is one of the biggest prison complexes in the world. It lies in the East River, nestled between Manhattan to the west, the Bronx to the north, and Queens to the south and east. Technically it is part of the Bronx, and technically it is not a prison, but a collection of ten jail facilities. The only access to the island is via the 1.3-kilometre Francis R. Buono Bridge, which leads from 15 Hazen Street, East Elmhurst in Queens, across the water to the southern side of the island.

It is one of the most violent 'prisons' in the United States, with a population of around 10,000 inmates. Mostly men. But there was always room for more, making it the perfect place to house the hundreds of temporally displaced illegal immigrants that had spontaneously appeared in the city.

When the truck finally stopped, and the doors opened, our travellers discovered theirs was one of dozens of transports destined for Rikers. A major military operation was underway, as soldiers and prison staff dressed in riot gear (which made them look like bipedal *Turtles*) opened the vehicles and bundled the new 'prisoners' off the transports for processing. Immediately, male and female refugees were separated, which prompted greater than expected anxiety for Ronan and Aliyah, Chase and Beth, and Edmund and Tiffany. After their adventures so far, and despite whatever friction there may have been, it felt somehow wrong not to be experiencing this new challenge together.

Male refugees were taken to the George R. Vierno Center (GRVC, or *'The Beacon'* for historical reasons), one of the most notorious jails at this most notorious of prisons. Female refugees were taken to the neighbouring and equally notorious Rose M. Singer Center (RMSC or *'Rosie's'*) – Riker's jail for women.

The Beacon housed some of the most violent and reprehensible male prisoners, but also had a sizable 'punitive segregation' block (we don't call it Solitary Confinement because officially that's not a thing). Here the new prisoners – who may or may not be 'dangerous' (another political waffle word) – could be kept separated; and if some native New Yorkers got caught up in it all, well, that was just collateral damage. It was a crude *hammer-and-nail* solution, but the city was in crisis.

Once separated by gender the refugees were marched into

167

their respective new homes. Soldiers served as crowd control, while General Wainwright stood on a platform barking orders through his megaphone.

'MKSR   ALLTHPRSNRS   RSRSSCHDND   PRPLY RGSTRD ...'

Despite no-one understanding a word he was saying, the troops knew the drill. They confiscated any obvious weapons – swords, spears, firearms, as well as armour and shields; also jewellery or coin or anything metallic that would trigger the detectors. Everyone was thoroughly patted down and anything deemed potentially dangerous taken from them.

The refugees came from disparate times and places, all classes and manner of dress. Everyone was confused and lost. Most were scared. Some responded aggressively or indignantly – a natural reaction to having a strange man in a bizarre uniform point a metallic weapon in your face while another fondled and stroked you all over; such as a French aristocrat from the 1800's who attempted to protest this abuse on their person. A spritz of pepper spray to the face quickly silenced him, leaving him a blubbering mess as he tried to wipe away the tears with an inadequate crocheted handkerchief.

But most of the new prisoners submitted willingly. They were used to being subjugated by one foreign army or another; this was just another in a long line of military adventures they had somehow got caught in the middle of. Also, most didn't speak English, or if they did it was of a more archaic form. For those that *did* have a chance at understanding the orders being barked at them, the unfamiliar American accents mutated the words into gibberish.

Some prisoners were combatants from a distant battle and were normally the ones doing the subjugation. They were not about to submit themselves to this kind of indignity. Genghis Khan himself, along with several of his Mongol horde, had landed in New York and was now causing no end of trouble for the soldiers and staff trying to wrangle the barbarian leader and his men. Pepper spray, bean bag shots and finally tasing were all used to quell the riot, though they had little effect on Khan himself and just seemed to make him angrier. It took ten men to wrestle the huge man to the ground and subdue him, with six handcuff cables required to secure his hands behind his back.

Amidst this organized bedlam, Ronan tried to get General Wainwright's attention 'General! General Wainwright! Remember us! I need to talk with you! *GENERAL*!'

A Turtle shoved Ronan back into line, tasing him for good measure. 'Welcome to Rikers Island. Now shut the fuck up.'

Ronan collapsed to the ground in jelly-legged spasms, though it only lasted a few seconds. Chase and Frimmel helped Ronan up, who continued to twitch uncontrollably.

A thunderous roar then filled the air as a plane took off from La Guardia with another load of people escaping New York. The runway was less than 100 meters away and they got a spectacular view of the Boeing 767 as it lifted into the air over the East River. Those who had never seen a plane – which was most of them – were astonished at this modern marvel; and the first few times it drew a chorus of awed *'Aahh's'* and fearful *'Ooohhh's.'* But planes were leaving so frequently that the travellers quickly got used to the miracle, and soon it was just another noisy distraction.

Something no-one quite got used to was the smell. The place stank of sewerage, fertilizer, and death. Several of the more refined travellers vomited the moment they stepped off the trucks. Others, such as those from Victorian London or Medieval Europe, who were used to such stench, appeared not to notice it. In fact, it made them feel right at home. Ronan and Chase in particular had to hold their noses against the pong, until they got inside.

'This is no good,' Chase said. 'By the time we get to speak to someone it'll be too late.'

'I did try,' Ronan twitched.

Once inside *The Beacon* they were confronted by a wall of bureaucrats wearing body armour, sitting at hastily erected tables, processing the new prisoners with paper and pen or laptop computer. They recorded personal details as best they could, took photos, and made assumptions; then directed the prisoner to a designated section where they would be grouped with like types for incarceration. Sections had been set up according to millennia (1600's, 1700's...), and within that, different regions (Europe, Asia, Africa...). These simple categories may have seemed logical, but were rife with complications as people from opposing sides in a war, or from different classes, or races, were bundled together as if they were all the same. And of course many were misattributed. An erroneous assumption would place a French-born man in Africa simply because he was black, or someone from Ancient Mesopotamia in Egypt because Mesopotamia wasn't a thing anymore and they didn't know how to spell it anyway (*messup Potato Mia? Messa Pot Aimie?*).

Despite the confusion, most of the prisoners did their best to adapt and cooperate. They could see they were all in the same boat, and this was not some random misfortune or divine torment (unless the gods were *really* messing with them). Rikers had become a spur-of-the-moment Ellis Island / Concentration Camp for accidental time travellers.

A large TV had been setup showing the news – another miracle that baffled most of the prisoners. A well-groomed young male reporter was giving a report live from outside the Apollo

Theater, as aerial footage of the Anomaly in Manhattan, as well as other locations around the world was shown. 'The latest position on the Inter-dimensional wormhole is north at West 125th Street and as far West as the New Jersey Turnpike. The George Washington Bridge is still open, though we expect that too will be consumed within a few hours. La Guardia Airport has additional flights leaving the city and is expected to continue operating until tomorrow when it will likely also be overtaken by the wormhole. Back to you, Amanda.'

'Thanks, Richard. We've just heard The Doomsday Clock, which is a way for scientists to measure how close we are to total Armageddon, has been set to Midnight. So, it's official folks. The end of the world is nigh. Stay tuned for more updates after this break.'

Then an ad for Liberty Life Insurance came on and everyone stopped paying attention.

General Wainwright meanwhile had moved inside. He continued bellowing incomprehensible orders through his megaphone, despite the fact that not only could no one understand him, no one could even hear him thanks to another plane leaving La Guardia.

'We have to do something,' Ronan said, then pointing at Wainwright. 'We're doomed if that guy's in charge.'

Wainwright looked directly at their group, as if he had heard Ronan. A soldier was pointing them out for some reason and within seconds they were surrounded by a contingent of armed men.

Wainwright stepped forward. He looked at Chase and Ronan. 'I know you. You're the ones who escaped our facility the other day when this all started.'

'To be fair,' Chase said, 'the security was pretty lax.'

'General. We know how to stop it. You have to let us go.'

Ronan was still twitching with uncontrollable spasms, so it was hard to take him seriously.

'For all I know you started this thing.'

'We did,' Chase admitted. 'And we've been trying to fix it ever since.'

Wainwright somehow felt he had tricked this confession out of Chase. 'So you admit it!' Then with uncanny cunning, 'You're from the future, aren't you?'

'How could you tell?' Ronan twitched. 'Is it the clothes?'

Wainwright held up the confiscated Pod.

Chase blinked.

Moments later Chase and Ronan found themselves in an interview room where they were sat down and told not to move. Wainwright sat opposite with two armed men standing behind him – just in case. You could never tell what other tricks these future people might have up their sleeves.

The Pod lay in the middle of the table.

'So what is it?' Wainwright asked.

'It's a Pod,' Chase explained. 'P.O.D. Programmable Omni-Functional Device.'

'What does it do?'

'Pretty much anything you want.'

'Like a smartphone.'

Ronan sniggered, then twitched.

'It's several generations past that,' Chase said diplomatically.

'Why doesn't it work?'

'It does. You just don't know how to use it.'

Chase reached for the Pod. The soldiers both raised their

M27 semi-automatics and trained them on Chase.

Chase withdrew his hand. 'It's not a weapon.'

'... Show me. Slowly.'

With the guns still aimed at him, Chase picked up the Pod, it instantly turned on thanks to the bio-security he had enabled. He called up the holo-display, selected the music app and played something from his personal playlist that seemed apropos for the moment. The strains of Vivaldi's *Four Seasons (Spring)* filled the room. The sound seemed to emanate from all around the room in a glorious virtual surround-scape.

'My phone can do that,' Wainwright said flatly.

Chase stroked the side of the Pod with his thumb, turning the music down, but kept it going as a calming soundtrack to their interrogation. 'It also translates.' He turned on the translator. 'Say something in another language.'

'I don't speak another language. I only speak American.'

Chase looked at the soldiers. 'Do either of you...?'

'Rodrigo,' Wainwright gestured. 'You speak Spanish, don't you? Say something in Spanish.'

'Like what?'

'I don't know. Anything.'

'I live in the Bronx and my mother makes a great quesadilla,' Rodrigo said.

'Say it in Spanish!'

'I did.'

Wainwright was confused. '... Say something else.'

'I like pizza, but not the ones that come from Little Ceasars.'

'In Spanish!' Wainwright demanded.

'That *was* in Spanish!' Rodrigo barked back, then added. 'Sir.'

The penny dropped. 'Oh. That's pretty good. What else does it do?' Wainwright snatched the Pod away from Chase. The holo-display deactivated. 'What happened?'

'It's coded to my DNA. Only I can use it.'

'Change it.'

'I can't,' Chase lied.

'Is this what you used to create that thing out there? That … Inter-Dimensional Wormhole that's destroying the city.'

'We call it a Doomsday Bubble,' Ronan said. His twitching having now subsided.

'Or Hellgate.'

'Or Giant Orb.'

'Or just The Anomaly.'

'Inter-Dimensional Wormhole is another good one,' Ronan said. 'Though to be accurate, it's more of a Trans-Temporal Wormhole.'

'And no, we didn't use the Pod to create it,' Chase said.

'For that we used a Time Machine,' Ronan finished.

'A time machine.' Wainwright couldn't believe he was having this conversation. 'So where is this time machine now?'

'Destroyed.'

'Devoured.'

'But we do know how to get rid of The Anomaly,' Chase was quick to add.

'We have to sing at it,' Ronan said.

'You're joking.'

'No sir, I am not joking.'

Chase started to explain. 'There's good reason to believe that on a quantum level, harmonious sound waves – '

' – Why the hell would you create something like that?!' Wainwright interrupted.

'Oh, we didn't mean to,' Chase said. 'It was an accident.'

'So all of this is because of some time travel experiment gone wrong?'

'Pretty much,' Ronan admitted.

Wainwright rose to his feet, incensed. 'Bloody boffins messing with the universe. You just can't leave things alone, can you? Always poking and prodding at creation, like it's your personal Lego set. Not a thought for the consequences. Like a pair of Frankensteins.'

Chase nodded agreement. 'Believe me, we get that now. But we have a way to fix it.'

'Singing at it?!' Wainwright's voice rose to a pitch not previously heard by anyone but his wife while at the height of orgasm. 'Give me a break!'

'What's your solution, then?' Ronan challenged.

'Nuke the fucker! President's given the order. We'd have done it by now if it wasn't for all these bloody tourists that keep popping out of it.'

'That'll only make it worse,' Chase told him.

'Says the guy who caused the problem in the first place. You've done enough damage.' He turned to the soldiers behind him. 'Find our guests here a nice secure cell for the rest of their short lives.'

CHAPTER 16
The Man in Black

Ronan and Chase were locked up in an eminently secure cell. Though they didn't know it yet Edmund, Frimmel and the male members of the Constantinople troupe were in neighbouring cells, as were Genghis Khan and his Mongol horde, along with a hundred or so other temporal refugees. Ronan looked about their tiny eggshell-white box with its tiny, barred window, two tiny metal bunks with inch-thin mattresses, and a large heavy steel door that could only be opened electronically by a master control.

'We're fucked.'

Chase had to agree.

Meanwhile, over in '*Rosie's*', Aliyah, Beth, Tiffany, Matilda and Hildegarde were likewise split across three separate cells and mixed in with a variety of women from other times and places. The 'methodical' processing that had taken place on arrival – where they assigned people to groups according to time period and region – was largely forgotten once they got to the actual cell block. Travellers were simply thrown into whatever empty cell was available, with no regard to their origin or language.

'Well, this sucks,' Aliyah declared as she looked about their tiny vomit-green box, with its tiny, barred window, two tiny metal bunks with inch-thin mattresses, and a large heavy steel door. 'Again!'

'Chase will come up with something,' Beth said confidently. 'Just you wait.'

Aliyah sighed and sat beside Beth. 'You like him, don't you?'

Beth nodded. 'It's the accent. Gets me every time.'

Aliyah smiled, thinking of Ronan. '...Yeah.'

Meanwhile, a suspiciously non-descript black car with blacked-out windows and somehow a blacked-out licence plate crossed the Francis R. Buono Memorial Bridge to Rikers Island and pulled up outside *The Beacon*. A man wearing an equally non-descript dark suit, with a long black trench-coat and shiny black shoes and carrying a black briefcase, stepped out of the car and marched towards the Center. He was a non-descript white guy, whose face was somehow completely obscured behind dark glasses. Your classic man in black. Indeed, the only bits of colour (if you could call it that) were the touches of grey salted into his temples and peppered through his unruly hair.

The man in black walked through the lobby of *The Beacon*, past all the travellers awaiting processing, and marched directly towards the rear office. He knew where he was going. He drew the gaze of some of the soldiers, but no-one dared interfere with him. Clearly, he was an important man. CIA or FBI, NSA or perhaps Secret Service. Without knocking, the man in black entered the room and closed the door firmly behind him.

'Who the hell are you?' Wainwright demanded.

The man in black produced his ID while removing his glasses, revealing his face. He was an older man, in his 70's, and looked vaguely familiar. He glanced at the Pod lying in the middle of the table, then back up at Wainwright and flashed his ID.

'Agent Herbert Wells. Interpol.'

'Interpol?'

'These *wormholes* are popping up all over the world, so of course we're taking an interest.'

'What do you want?'

The man in black placed the briefcase on the table, opened it, and produced a folder with a red cover. He handed it to Wainwright.

'This is a Red Notice for fourteen people you have detained here. They are to be handed over into my custody.'

Wainwright opened the folder revealing photos of Chase, Ronan, Aliyah and Beth, plus Edmund, Frimmel, Tiffany and the rest of the troupe.

Wainwright pushed back. He didn't take orders from *Interpol*. 'What makes you think they're here?'

'Oh, come now, General. Let's not play games.'

'You've got no authority here. This is a military operation. The President has declared Martial Law.'

'Ah... State of Emergency, sir,' Rodrigo corrected.

Wainwright waved this away. 'That *thing* out there is in direct violation of homeland security. I have orders from the President himself to detain all undocumented historical aliens that enter this city. So I ain't releasin' shit to you, Mister Interpol.'

The man in black glanced again at the Pod on the table. 'Do you have any idea what's going on out there, General? This is bigger than micro-managing a few illegal immigrants.'

'I have my orders. And I'm pretty sure my boss outranks whoever the fuck your boss is.'

'You want to send these people back where they came from, don't you? I can help you do that.'

'I don't need your help. We've got the situation under control.'

178

'I doubt it.'

The man in black glanced again at the Pod. He clearly wanted it. Wainwright picked it up. 'Looks like a remote, doesn't it? Or a robot dildo for midgets.'

'Sure it's not a toy?' the man in black said. 'It looks like a toy.'

'It's a weapon.'

'Nah,' the man in black scoffed. 'I've seen these before. It's a toy for kids. You know, like a lightsaber.'

'Then why do you keep looking at it?' Wainwright asked.

'I was just wondering what it's doing on your desk.'

'We took it off one of the prisoners. In fact, one of the ones in your little portfolio here.' Wainwright flipped to Chase's picture. He looked back up at the man in black who was putting his dark glasses back on. Then Wainwright looked back at the picture. Then back at the man. 'Hang on a sec'.'

The man in black snatched the Pod out of Wainwright's hand. It instantly came to life and with a quick flick of the thumb the holo-display appeared floating above the device. As Wainwright and the soldiers lunged toward the man in black – who they now recognised as an older Chase – he selected a function and a blinding *flash* filled the room.

Seconds later old Chase exited the room. 'Oh, I've missed you,' he told the Pod as he crossed the crowded lobby making for the guard's station.

Wainwright and the soldiers emerged from the interview room ten seconds later – dazed and temporarily blinded. But it was already too late. Old Chase had selected *AR Projection* from the Pod menu and chosen the *Monkey Rampage* preset. As Wainwright emerged from the interview room hundreds of monkeys appeared in the rafters. They leapt down, landing on furniture, climbing pillars, and seemingly attacking everyone in the building.

It was mayhem.

The monkeys were, of course, an Augmented Reality holographic projection – completely harmless. But they looked real. And sounded real. And to have an angry horde of monkeys descend on you from the ceiling (real or otherwise) was terrifying. The fact that most of them were macaques didn't help either, with their razor-like canines and dreadful bird-like screeches.

People desperately swatted at the formless creatures but their blows passed right through them. Everyone – travellers, soldiers and prison staff alike – stampeded for the exit in a mad panic.

Old Chase anticipated this reaction; indeed, it was exactly what he was hoping for. So while everyone was running out of the building, he calmly walked in the opposite direction, grabbed the keys from the wall of the guards room where he knew they would be hanging, and walked on toward the cell blocks.

Ronan and Chase sat opposite each other, heads practically butting in their non-spacious 6-foot by 8-foot eggshell-white cell with the tiny, barred window and large metal door. 'We're fucked,' Ronan repeated.

Chase still had to agree.

'Not only are *we* fucked, but the world is fucked. The entire universe is fucked. We managed to fuck up the entire universe. All because we wanted to go to a party and meet Steven Hawking.'

'It was my fault,' Chase admitted gloomily. 'I should have seen this in the math. Too many unknown variables. Too many infinities.'

'No. It's my fault,' Ronan said. 'You wouldn't have made the damn thing if I hadn't given you the idea and urged you on. I'm responsible.'

Chase laughed a little. 'Well, in a day or two it won't matter. No-one will remember.'

'Because there'll be no one left *to* remember.'

'Worst part is, I finally met a girl I like,' Chase said.

'Beth?'

'Yeah.'

'Me too.'

'Who?'

'Aliyah, of course.'

'Oh.'

'Who'd have thought,' Ronan said. 'Americans.'

'Yeah,' Chase agreed. 'Something about the accent.'

A long silence followed as both became lost in their thoughts, imagining what might have been.

A plane took off from La Guardia and the building trembled...

Their heavy metal door *buzzed*, startling them both. Without rising, Ronan reached over and gently pushed against the door – it squeaked open.

They exited their cell to discover all the other cells had likewise been remotely opened. Everyone slowly emerged and gathered in the common room – fellow travellers, and regular inmates of *The Beacon* dressed in Bob Barker green jumpsuits. Those in the upper levels made their way downstairs. Chase and Ronan spotted Edmund and Frimmel coming down the stairs and gravitated to them; they were surprisingly pleased to reunite with their accidental companions. Everyone was milling about, sitting at the metal benches, trying to remain inconspicuous and not stare.

The jail was normally run by *bloods*, a gang of black men identifiable by their red bandanas, and who clearly had control over the other inmates. Normally they would have held dominion over the whole common room, but the new arrivals (notably the Mongols) were a challenge to their authority. The situation was so bizarre though, that no-one quite knew what to do. So the *bloods* gathered on one side of the room, while the Mongols claimed the other half. Genghis Khan, despite not having any weapons or armour, was a formidable presence; and with his horde gathered around him on one side, and the *bloods* facing them from across the room, everyone else instinctively moved to the neutral edges of the space or 'picked a side' based on where they felt safest. All of this happened without a word being uttered. Even the innocent among them – those who had never before encountered such a confrontation – quickly worked out the rules of the game and found a way to hide themselves in the crowd.

The air in the room was heavy with a silent dread. Everyone warily eyed everyone else. It was as if the entire history of man, and his longing for power and subjugation, had been reduced to a tiny room on a tiny island in the middle of a vanishing city, and yet the primal instinct for dominion persisted. And if conquest was not possible then destruction was always an option. Civilisation was an illusion. Man was, and always had been, a selfish, stupid, violent beast.

But then, the leader of the *bloods* – an intense young man by the name of 'Sly' (because, despite Stalone, the name Sylvester still sounded like a dork) with some rather impressive tattoos across his upper body – stepped forward and defiantly claimed the centre of the room. His crew followed and took up position behind him. Khan stepped forward to meet the young man, his Mongol horde following like a Kardashian entourage, and the two men were face to face.

Khan was much, much larger than the scrawny (some might say *wiry*) young black man facing him, but Sly held his ground. Each in their way were equally intimidating, and there seemed a mutual respect between the two men.

Sly extended his hand. Khan took it and they shook.

Everyone relaxed.

In that moment the two leaders set aside their personal ambitions for a greater good. Neither knew what that greater good was, but clearly something was happening that was more important than their little turf wars, and they needed to face it together.

Sly addressed the crowd. 'Does any motherfucker here know what the fuck is going on?'

Chase and Ronan looked at each other.

'Well…' Ronan ventured, and all eyes turned on him. 'We… might have had a little something to do with it.'

Khan approached Ronan. Ronan backed up against the wall, fearing he was about to be pummelled, but Khan stopped before him, reached into his leather vest and pulled out … a beer bottle.

'Hey, that's our bottle!' Ronan declared.

'Ene chiniikh?' said Khan as he offered it to him .

Ronan took the bottle, nodding. 'Yeah. How did you get it?' He looked inside. 'And what happened to the note?'

Khan grabbed Ronan by the shirt with one hand and lifted him off the ground. Nose to nose, Khan quietly threatened: 'A yaagaad namaig dainy talbaraas khulgailj ene gazar avchirsan yum be? Chi khen be?!'

'I'm sorry,' Ronan squeaked. 'I don't speak barbarian.'

'Ta bidnees yuu khüsch baigaagaa kheleerei! Esvel bi bolno

gut you like a pig and leave your entrails in the sun to fester and rot while you still breath!'

'You're speaking English! He's speaking English!'

'What are you talking about?' Khan said.

'Hey,' Frimmel cried. 'I can understand you all again.'

Then they heard a strange stampeding rumble approach. It was screeching and caterwauling and getting closer. Everyone froze, even Khan who was still holding Ronan in mid-air. Prison guards could be heard firing their beanbag guns and tasers, and then fleeing in terror when the weapons did absolutely nothing to deter what they faced.

'What is that?' Frimmel asked, terrified.

Chase recognised the sound. 'Rampaging Monkeys,' he said, then smiled, because he knew – or at least believed he knew – who was coming.

On hearing the terrifying bird-like screeches of the creatures, Khan added: 'Fucking macaques.' He lowered Ronan as the monkeys appeared racing down the corridor outside the main entrance to the cell block. In the middle of the corridor, unconcerned by the monkeys rampaging about him, walked a man dress all in black.

Despite there being a barred door between them and the corridor of monkeys, everyone instinctively moved to the sides of the common room, clearing a path for the creatures should they bust through the barrier.

But there was no busting. The monkeys rampaged right through the bars, down the middle of the common room, swinging on railings and leaping up and over the stairs on their way through. Everyone in the middle of the room parted like a fearful sea, clearing a path for the creatures.

The man in black unlocked the barred door and entered

the room, monkeys swirling all around him, and yet he remained miraculously untouched. The creatures rampaged right through the opposite wall and disappeared, their howls fading as another plane took off from La Guardia and drowned them out. The man in black remained standing alone in the middle of the room, while everyone else hugged the walls.

Chase (that is: young Chase) stepped forward to greet the man in black (Old Chase). 'Nicely played.'

Ronan stepped forward, adjusting his shirt. 'What is it with the goddamned monkeys?!'

'I thought you'd appreciate the irony,' the man in black said as he removed his glasses.

'Hey. I know you.'

'Hi Ronan. It's been a long time.'

'... Chase?' Ronan did a double take between the two Chase's. 'He's you. You're him. But Old. Like really old. What happened to you?'

'Time,' was all old Chase said.

'Ha! Time,' Ronan laughed. 'I get it. Wait? Seriously?'

Young Chase smiled. 'I knew you were me the moment I heard the monkeys. No-one else can use the Pod, after all.'

Old Chase offered the device to young Chase, who raised a hand in refusal. 'No, you hang on to it. I think you have a better idea what needs to be done.'

'I don't understand what's happening?' Frimmel said.

'Neither do I,' Edmund told him. 'But just go with it. It usually works out.'

Sly, who had run in a panic from the monkeys like everyone else (everyone but the fearless Khan), finally found his testicles. 'What the actual fuck, old man?!'

'I'm sorry for startling you all,' old Chase told everyone. 'But the illusion was necessary to secure your escape.'

'You breakin' us outta here?' Sly asked.

'My intention was just the new arrivals,' old Chase said, then addressing those in the green jumpsuits, 'but you're all welcome to come along and save the world with us. We could use the numbers.'

'What if we don't wanna?' one of them asked aggressively, as he was not inclined to trust an old white guy dressed in black and looking too much like an overpaid cop.

'The choice is yours,' old Chase told them. Then addressing the travellers among them. 'As for the rest of you, I promise we'll get you all back to your own times; back to where you came from.'

'You can return us to the battle?' Khan asked.

'Yes,' old Chase assured him. 'I have seen it.'

'Old you is pretty cool,' Ronan said to Chase the younger. 'Where did that come from?'

'Follow me!' old Chase charged with a wave as he headed out the cell block.

In *Rosie's* all the cell doors opened with a loud *buzz,* and as the women emerged into their common area, they could see their men at the end of the central corridor, led by a mysterious man in black.

'I knew you'd think of something,' Beth said once she was reunited with Chase.

'It wasn't me,' Chase told her, then pointing to the man in black: 'It was him.'

'Same diff,' old Chase said.

Beth looked at the older man, confused.

'Hi Beth,' he said fondly.

'...Chase?'

'Freaky, huh?' Ronan said.

'How old are you?' Beth asked.

'Seventy-two.'

'Are we...? I mean, did I...?'

'I can't tell you.'

Beth was annoyed. 'You mean you *won't* tell me.'

Old Chase just smiled knowingly. 'Don't worry, it all works out. After all, I'm here, aren't I?'

'How can there be two of you?' Aliyah asked.' Doesn't that break some kind of time travel rule?'

'Paradoxes are not meant be explained,' Chase the younger told her. 'They're meant to be enjoyed.'

Aliyah was not satisfied with this flippant response. 'I thought you were supposed to be the smart one.'

'Sometimes logic just doesn't work and you have to go with your gut,' old Chase added.

'Trust your instincts,' Beth said.

'Exactly,' Chase agreed.

Aliyah, still not satisfied, asked the man in black. 'I just wanna know how you got here?'

'I am here because I need to be here, and because you need me to be here. If I were not, then I could not, because you will have failed. But as I am, then you did not, do not, because I am here.'

Aliyah blinked. 'I'm sorry I asked.'

'Don't be sorry for that,' old Chase told her. 'As with any good paradox, it's the question that matters, not the answer.'

'Cool, and wise,' Ronan said to Chase the younger, impressed with his friend's growth. Chase was a little jealous of his older self. It was an odd feeling.

They reached the main entrance to *Rosie's* where they found the rest of the men waiting. The place was surprisingly deserted otherwise. No guards. No soldiers. They had all fled after the monkey rampage. Yet most of the trucks remained. Abandoned.

The prisoners watched as another plane took off from La Guardia, burdened with refugees on their way to Australia. To the west, they could see the crest of the Anomaly as it continued to consume Manhattan.

'Come on,' Old Chase said. 'We don't have much time.'

'Ha!' Ronan exclaimed. 'Time!'

Khan and his men found the truck where their weapons and armour had been stashed. They reclaimed their property and were once again a warrior force to be reckoned with.

Old Chase led the march to the bridge – the only way off Rikers Island. There was about a thousand men, women and children from different eras, along with some existing Rikers inmates (both male and female) who had decided to join in and help. Wherever and whenever they had come from, they were united in a single cause – to stop Doomsday and get back home.

Awaiting them on the bridge was General Wainwright and the US army. There were tanks, artillery, and rows and rows of armed soldiers blocking their path on the long, narrow road. Undaunted, the Rikers prisoner army marched onto the bridge to meet them.

Ten meters from the front line of soldiers, old Chase raised his hand and the march halted. Wainwright stood atop one of the tanks. He pulled out his trusty megaphone.

'NOW LISTEN UP ALL OF YOU. YOU ARE IN DIRECT VIOLATION OF AN EXECUTIVE ORDER FROM THE PRESIDENT OF THE UNITED STATES. TURN AROUND AND RETURN TO YOUR CELLS IMMEDIATELY, AND NONE OF

YOU WILL BE HARMED.'

'He must have got his megaphone fixed,' Ronan said. 'I can actually understand him.'

'The Pod's translating,' Chase the younger explained.

'Oh.'

'DO YOU HEAR ME? TURN AROUND AND GO BACK. NOW!'

Old Chase nodded to Khan. Khan and his Mongol horde stepped forward and formed a front line of defence – shields raised and weapons at the ready.

'REALLY? YOU DON'T STAND A CHANCE YOU HEATHEN RELICS. THIS IS THE U.S. ARMY WE'RE TALKIN' ABOUT.'

Khan growled. These Americans were just as arrogant as the Chinese.

'Patience, my friend,' old Chase told Khan. He then triggered the Pod's holo-display and made a selection.

'I REPEAT – TURN AROUND AND RETURN TO YOUR CELLS NOW!'

There was a brief pause as Wainwright and his soldiers waited anxiously. They had superior fire power, but most had never been in an actual battle before; and they didn't relish facing the Mongol army of Genghis Khan armed swords and spears in close-quarters combat.

There was movement in the prisoner ranks – a bustle around the ankles of the frontline Mongols. Everyone tensed, then they saw emerging from between and around the prisoner's feet ... kittens and puppies.

The most adorable kittens and puppies they had ever seen. Dozens of them ... hundreds! They gamboled, skittered and bounded across the divide between the two armies.

They were *SOOOOO cute*! The soldiers didn't know how to react. They couldn't fire on kittens and puppies!

'It's a trick!' Wainwright shouted at them. 'Remember the monkeys!! They're not real!!' He raised the megaphone to his mouth. 'REMEMBER THE MONKEYS!'

The adorable creatures reached the ankles of the frontline soldiers, who were entranced as the animals cooed, purred and yapped at their ankles. The soldiers lowered their weapons. Some tried to stroke and pat the animals, and although holograms, they still reacted to the 'touch' like a real animal would.

SOOOOOOO CUTE!

The tiny creatures continued moving through the ranks unhindered. Leaping up onto the tanks and climbing adorably all over their weapons. The soldiers were spellbound.

'Pull yourselves together, goddammit!' Wainwright ordered. 'This isn't a petting zoo!'

Wainwright discovered a kitten had climbed his tank and was now directly in front of him. It meowed adorably. He eyed it suspiciously. Tried to brush it away. 'Piss off, cat.' His hand just passed right through it. It meowed again.

Old Chase watched as Wainwright tried to shoo away the kitten. He tapped the Pod display, and the kitten transformed, growing into an enormous lion. Instead of a meow this time it *ROOOAAARED*!!!

Wainwright shit himself (figuratively and quite possibly literally); and despite knowing full well the creature was not real, he screamed in terror.

All the other kittens and puppies likewise transformed into ferocious versions of themselves: Lions, Tigers, Panthers, Cougars, as well as Dire Wolves, Rottweilers, Giant Pit-bulls, and even a few three-headed Cerberuses and Black Shucks from mythology. Most were huge, vicious creatures. But there were also some smaller yet equally ferocious feral dogs and cats in the mix. These ones tended to go for the face.

'Fall Back! Fall Back!' Wainwright screamed as his lion leapt into action. '*AHHHH!*' He dropped into his tank and closed the hatch.

The U.S. army fled for their lives, abandoning their posts and their weapons, leaping over the side of the bridge into the surrounding water, or running to the rear towards the mainland.

Wainwright, now safely nestled inside his tank, breathed a sigh of relief. Then he turned to discover two more wild beasts in the cab with him. Screaming a scream that had hitherto been unheard by anyone in existence (including his wife) Wainwright scrambled desperately for the hatch.

Meanwhile, on the bridge, old Chase nodded to Khan – *Now.*

Khan grinned. 'Finally.' He raises his sword. *'KHALDLAGA!!!!!!'*

Khan and his Mongol horde were unleashed. They charged the army lines shouting at full voice.

The other prisoners – travellers and inmates alike – brought up the rear, adding their voices to the deafening battle cry.

The few dedicated soldiers who managed to stay at their post despite the holographic beasts, now faced a wall of very real Mongols armed with primitive, but nevertheless brutally efficient, weapons. It was too much. They followed their comrades, leaping into the river or making a tactical retreat back to Queens.

Wainwright emerged from his tank, got one glimpse of the Mongols approaching, then scrambled to the pavement and ran for his life to the mainland. 'Retreat!! Retreat!!!!'

Khan raised his sabre and was about to drive it into the head of one of the soldiers.

'Stop!' old Chase commanded. 'Remember what we agreed!'

Khan stayed his hand. 'Just this one. I need to kill something.'

'When you get back to your own time you can kill as many as you like,' old Chase told him. 'This man is not your enemy!'

Khan grumbled... then turned the tip of the sabre onto old Chase. 'If we do not get back, I will kill you. Very slowly.'

'Fair enough.'

Their path clear, the prisoners crossed the Francis R. Buono Memorial Bridge and headed west.

CHAPTER 17

Time is on My Side

Once over the bridge, the Rikers escapees continued up Hazen Street, then turned right onto Grand Central Parkway. This would lead them over Randalls Island – where they came dangerously close to the growing Anomaly as it encroached into the Harlem river – before turning north and into the Bronx via the Major Deegan Expressway. The Anomaly had by now consumed all Lower Manhattan, as well as parts of Jersey and Brooklyn. Harlem and South Bronx would be next.

'So what now?' Chase the younger asked.

'Aliyah knows,' old Chase replied.

'I do?'

'Where's the best place to gather the most people together, and which is right in the path of that thing?' Old Chase pointed to the Anomaly.

'Ah,' Aliyah nodded. It was obvious.

There were two secular religions in New York City: theatre and baseball. Aliyah was of the theatre persuasion, but she had been to enough games thanks to her father and a string of ill-conceived boyfriends, to appreciate the latter. In New York you were either a Yankees fan or a Mets fan – unless it was the Boston Red Sox they were versing, then you were a New York fan regardless. Aliyah was a Yankees fan, that's how her father had trained her, and Yankee Stadium in South Bronx was their home.

Old Chase handed Aliyah her iPhone.

'How did you get my phone?' Old Chase just smiled at her. 'Never mind.' Aliyah made a call, starting with: 'Hey, Owen... Yeah, I'm fine. Listen, Got a job for you and Clive ...'

'You scrub up pretty well as an old man,' Beth said to Chase the younger.

'Thanks.'

'So I guess when this is all over, you'll be going back.'

Chase looked at her. 'Back?'

'To your own time.'

'I guess.'

'Can I come with you?' Beth asked, like it was just around the corner.

Chase was taken aback. '... Are you sure that's what you want?'

'I'm sure.'

Chase wanted Beth to go with him but didn't think it fair to ask. Even now that it was her idea, he wasn't sure it was a good idea. 'What if...' he looked at his older self. 'What if I'm not going back to my own time?'

Beth also then glanced at old Chase marching beside them. As if on cue he turned and looked her dead in the eye, then smiled fondly – as if remembering this moment. Beth turned back to Chase the younger. 'I don't mind where we go, as long as we go together.' As an answer, Chase took Beth's hand. They walked hand in hand the rest of the way.

Aliyah, having made the necessary calls, hung up the phone. 'It's all arranged,' she told old Chase. 'They'll meet us there.'

'Good.'

Ronan saw his moment. 'Aliyah?'

'Hmm?'

'Um... when this is all over. I mean, assuming we succeed and the universe doesn't get swallowed up by a SpaceTime Anomaly that I helped create... you know... if we're still here tomorrow, and for the foreseeable future – '

'– Spit it out, Ronan.'

Why was this so hard? Usually Ronan had no trouble talking to women. 'Um... You wanna hang out?'

'Hang out?'

'Yeah, you know... Hang out sometime.'

'Like go on a date?'

'Yeah, you could call it that... I guess.'

'How will that work,' Aliyah asked. 'With me here and you back in 2100?'

'Well... I was thinking. What if I stayed?'

'You'd stay? For me?'

'Yeah, I mean... if you were cool with that.'

'You'd give up your chance to get back home just to go on a date with me?'

'Well... yeah. I mean... of course. You're awesome.'

Aliyah smiled. He was adorable. And the accent was to die for.

'But you gotta promise me one thing,' Ronan stressed. 'You're not allowed to hit me anymore.'

By way of answer, Aliyah 'punched' him gently on the shoulder.

'Okay, maybe... just a little.'

Meanwhile, Edmund and Frimmel walked alongside each other in silence. Frimmel was eating a packet of peanuts he managed to somehow find back at the jail. He offered one to Edmund. 'Peanut?'

'Thank you.'

'So you're from the middle ages,' Frimmel said.

'In the year of our Lord ten-eighty-six. And you're from Germany?'

'Nineteen Twenty-Three.'

'Hans, isn't it?'

'Yes.'

'Edmund. How do you do?' They shook. Edmund introduced his new girlfriend to his left. 'This is Tiffany.'

'Hello Tiffany,' Frimmel waved.

'I'm from Constantinople,' Tiffany said. 'In the year twelve-oh-four. Though I come originally from York.' Tiffany then proceeded to introduce the rest of her troupe who were walking nearby.

'Hans,' Hildegarde asked once they were introduced. 'Do you have a girlfriend?'

'Yes, I do,' Frimmel told her, unaware Hildegarde was flirting with him. 'Her name is Ilsa. I hope to return to her very soon.'

Hildegarde, only slightly disappointed, nodded understanding.

Then after a short pause, as if realising what had just happened, Frimmel turned to Hildegarde. 'Peanut?'

After a couple of hours the march approached its goal – Yankee Stadium. The Anomaly loomed behind them, encroaching from the South-West. Hundreds of other New Yorkers were likewise converging on the stadium. Owen, Clive and their vast network of friends and colleagues had spread the word via social media and thousands of people were turning up for the impromptu 'Save the World' concert.

The travellers entered through Gate 4, which led them into the great hall, a massive space with a high ceiling and festooned with banners of players past. This was the new Yankee Stadium, barely a decade old, pristine as the day it opened, and a very impressive architectural achievement. It was the biggest building many of the travellers had ever seen outside of a cathedral. Already the hall was filling up with spectators for the show. People were excited, anxious, and hopeful.

Aliyah led the march through the great hall, under the Legends seating area and directly out onto the stadium grounds. In short order a stage was being setup at the northern end of the field, with a massive PA and lighting rig. Normally this would take a couple of days to construct, but with every capable stagehand and technician in New York on the job, it was getting done in just a few hours. This was the most important show any of them had ever worked on, and it might just be their last. They were going to save the world with music or go out with a bang.

The cream of Broadway had turned up, along with local rock, pop, jazz or classical performers; after all, this was the home of Julliard, Carnegie Hall and Electric Lady Studios. Among them was the singer who had come to be known simply as *Yeshua,* the front man for one of the biggest bands of the 60s and 70s – *The Electric Garden.* He was 80 years old now but could still rock out with the best of them; and he looked good in leather jacket and jeans.

As the travellers entered, Yeshua gave Chase, Beth and Frimmel each in turn a big hug. 'I thought I'd never see you guys again!' he said in perfect Americanised English. 'You changed my life.' Then he noticed old Chase, realised who he was, and gave him a hug too. 'No need to explain,' he told them. 'I'm sure it all makes sense somehow.'

As night fell, and the Anomaly encroached, an impromptu band setup on stage, with the musicians from the Constantinople troupe joining in, as well as the orchestra from the Titanic, and a left-handed guitarist by the name of Jimi. 'Hey guys. Mind if I sit in?'

Clive served as Director for the show, while Owen was Musical Director, shepherding a large chorus of musical theatre luminaries to the stage, including the cast from Aliyah's ill-fated production of *The Time Machine*. Aliyah gave Clive and Owen a big hug. 'This is amazing! How did you pull it together so quickly?'

'It's New York, sweetie,' Owen said. 'Put the word out and they come a runnin'.'

'Any excuse for a show,' Clive added. 'Especially when it might be their last.'

Aliyah found herself standing next to Bernadette, Audra, and Patti; even Julie, Liza and Barbra were there, along with Jeremy, Lin, Nathan, Mandy and dozens more stage legends both past and present. Everyone who was anyone had turned up to help. With this many stars on the one stage there were some minor 'personality' issues and rivalries they had to navigate (being mindful who stood next to whom, and whether they were at the front or the back of the ensemble), but Clive, the consummate diplomat, was equal to the challenge. So many great performers had come that not everyone could fit on the stage, so risers were brought in and a new tier was created along the front of the stage.

The rest of the Rikers Army – travellers and prisoners alike – joined the thousands of other spectators gathering on the empty field or filling the stands. Khan and his Mongol horde, weapons at the ready, lined up around the foot of the stage as security, just in case anyone got any ideas. Memories of *Altamont* crossed the minds of some of the older patrons, but hopefully this would be more of a Monterey/Woodstock experience.

With the stage set, lighting quickly rigged, and the performers mostly in place, all they were waiting on was sound. Clive turned to their mix engineer standing behind the monitor console at the side of stage. 'Hey Pab! ETA?'

Pab held up five fingers. 'We got time for a sound check!' he called.

'I doubt it!' Clive answered.

'No worries.'

Meanwhile, outside Yankee Stadium, General Wainwright and the U.S. Army approached the venue in transports, tanks and on foot. They took up positions at each of the gates, blocking anyone else from entering; though there were already about 60,000 people inside, so they were a little late to the party.

General Wainwright stood on his tank overseeing the action and barking orders at his troops. "CVRLL THEXTS. WRGNNTRPM NSYYD!'

Tanks flanked each corner of the stadium, canons aimed directly into the Gates. Yankee Stadium was under siege. Behind them, the Anomaly grew. So while the tanks faced the venue, the soldiers warily watched the spherical vortex of destruction as it made directly for them.

Within the stadium, the field and stands were filled with travellers, New Yorkers and anyone else from the tristate area who was within range and got the call. The stands on the south-western side were kept deliberately empty, the Anomaly visible just over the top of the stadium walls at the Gate 4 entrance.

The PA came to life with the sound of feedback. Pab said a quick 'ONE, TWO' into his console mic to test it, then gave Clive the thumbs up. They were ready to rock.

Aliyah stepped forward and tapped the Mic. 'Hello? Can you all hear me?'

A cheer went up from the crowd surrounding her that was positively deafening. It reminded her of the day her father took her to Opening Day in 2012 and they witnessed Carlos Pena hit a Grand Slam. Aliyah had never played to such a massive crowd before. It was both terrifying and exhilarating.

Swallowing her heart which had leapt into her throat, Aliyah continued. 'Hi everyone. Thanks for coming out … and helping us save the world.'

Another great cheer went up.

'So here's what we're gonna do. We're gonna sing that thing into oblivion.'

Another great cheer.

'So when the... bubble reaches us here, I need you all to stay calm, and sing at the top of your lungs. Okay?'

Another cheer; and then a chant – *Sing, Sing, Sing, Sing…*

Aliyah turned to the 200-piece band/orchestra and 100-person ensemble behind her. 'You guys ready?'

Owen had his baton raised. 'Just tell me when, sweetie.'

Just then the Anomaly entered the stadium, eating through the south-western stands, its bulbous crest swelling like a massive Blob of destruction. It ate through the raked seating on its approach to the field and home base.

Everyone was stunned for a moment and pulled back. Those

on the field quickly realised they were in the front line and started to push back towards the stage.

'Stay calm everyone, please,' Aliyah reassured, her voice booming over the PA and echoing off the far walls. Then turning away from the mic: 'Hit it, Owen!'

Owen, who had also become momentarily stunned by the looming Anomaly, recovered his senses. He turned to the orchestra, raised his arms, and gave them a downbeat.

The orchestra started playing *Time is on My Side* (by Jerry Ragovoy), made famous by The Rolling Stones. Jimi was on lead guitar and gave a blistering 4-bar intro; and then the ensemble belted out the first chorus. As soon as the crowd heard and recognised the tune they joined in, and the entire stadium was singing it:

'Ti-i-i-ime is on my side. Yes, it is.'

Instantly, the Anomaly responded to the music with a kaleidoscopic display of colour and movement. It pulsed and swirled and stopped dead in its tracks.

Yeshua joined Aliyah at the mic. They each took a breath and launched into the first verse: *'Now you alwa – '*

– The PA shut down.

Everything went abruptly quiet. Everyone was stunned. The crowd let out a great collective moan.

Aliyah turned to Clive. 'What happened?'

Clive turned to Pab in a panic.

Pab threw his arms up in a controlled freak-out. He had no idea.

Everyone turned to the Anomaly, which had stopped swirling and began to grow again.

Then ear-splitting feedback screeched from the PA and they heard:

TAP TAP TAP.

'Am I on?... Are you sure? I can't hear anything.' It was Wainwright. Somehow, he had hijacked the sound system.

TAP TAP TAP

Khan growled. He signalled his Mongol horde and they raced off in search of the General.

'Sorry to interrupt your little singalong, folks,' Wainwright blasted patronisingly over the PA. 'But you're all under arrest. No one move. And ahh – Mister Interpol, if you're out there, that includes you.'

Backstage, General Wainwright was at the main snake splitter (the big box that all the stage mics were plugged into). The two soldiers who had somehow been drafted into being Wainwright's bodyguard stood with him. Rodrigo, who had a background in audio engineering, was responsible for shutting down the PA and giving Wainwright the hand mic he now used to address the Stadium.

'All the prisoners and illegals who escaped from Rikers Island, we have transports waiting outside to take you all back. I suggest you cooperate. My men have orders this time to kill anyone who causes trouble, and … Oh, shit!'

Wainwright had spotted Khan and his Mongol horde approaching.

"**KHALDLAGA!!!!!!**' Khan cried and the Mongols *charged!*

Rodrigo and his fellow bodyguard ran in the opposite direction.

Wainwright was frozen to the spot.

In the stadium, everyone listened as the PA broadcast the sounds of the melee backstage. There was the sound a mic being dropped, followed by the high-pitched squeal of a girl (or so it sounded).

Then followed a moment of silence… then:

'Put it back the way it was,' came Kahn's resonant voice.

'Ahh... sure thing,' said Rodrigo. 'Please don't kill me!'

'*GRRRR!*'

There was a loud clunk from the PA. Pab gave a thumbs up.

'Let's try that again,' Aliyah said into her mic.

The orchestra started the song again. The ensemble belted out the chorus and the Anomaly swirled and pulsed in sympathetic vibrations. This time as the verse came round Yeshua and Aliyah got to sing. And as the chorus came back around everyone now knew it, no matter what time they were from, and the whole stadium sang along:

'Ti-i-i-ime is on my side, yes it is!'

English football fans had a habit of singing popular songs en-masse, like *Don't Look Back in Anger* by Oasis, or *We are the Champions* by Queen. But the intensity of those massive chants paled in comparison to this ensemble of New Yorkers, Rikers Island prisoners, and temporal refugees. The stadium positively shook with the sound of sixty-thousand voices at full harmonious roar.

The Anomaly, awash with swirling colours, began to shrink. And as Jimi stepped forward to play a blistering lead break, its progress increased.

Ronan and Chase, who were on the field with all the other Travelers, began to usher them all into the Anomaly, sending them home. 'Join hands with those you love!' Ronan told them all. 'Stick together until you come out the other side!'

'And just keep thinking to yourself: There's no place like home!' Chase added.

Still singing, groups of travellers linked in chains both long and short, dashed into the Anomaly to be swallowed up by the swirling sphere. Hundreds of them charging headlong back to their own times.

As the song neared its end the orchestra transitioned into *The Time Warp* (by Richard O'Brien) from *The Rocky Horror Show*.

Jimi, the musicians from the Titanic, the Constantinople troupe, and any other travellers that were on the stage, stepped off to join the others on their way home.

'Great vibe, man,' Jimi told Owen as he left. 'Let's do it again sometime.'

'Let's do the Time Warp again. Let's do the Time Warp again...'

The Anomaly was shrinking ever faster. Its front remained within the bounds of Yankee Stadium, as if the surface assaulted by the music was frozen in place, and the rest of the giant Hellgate was pulled in behind it, withering down to the size of a ten-storey building. Travellers dived headlong into the Doomsday Bubble. Khan and his Mongol horde charged in, weapons raised and ready, as they returned to their ancient battle.

'Tiffany, come on!' cried Bapoo.

'I'm staying with Edmund,' she told them.

'You are?' Edmund said.

'You don't want me to?'

'Of course. But – '

Bapoo stepped forward and gave them both a reassuring hug. 'Good luck to the both of you.' The rest of the troupe joined in for a group hug to farewell their beloved Tiffany. Then holding hands, they all entered the Bubble and vanished from 2018.

Ronan, Chase, Beth, Edmund, Tiffany and Frimmel stood by what remained of the Anomaly, now shrunk to the size of a two-story house. Most of the travellers had departed, though a few lingered to say their own farewells. The field was almost empty.

Aliyah left the stage, leaving the song in the capable hands of Jeremy, Lin and the Broadway ensemble, and joined her compatriots on the field. Meanwhile, old Chase stood back and watched the group from a discrete distance. He knew how this played out.

Edmund took Tiffany's hand and turned to the others. 'Are you sure this will return us to ten-eighty-six?'

'Absolutely,' Ronan said.

'Almost certainly,' Chase added.

'Almost?'

'That's Quantum Physics for you. You never quite know how it's gonna land.'

'Just take a run at it,' Ronan told them.

'Trust your gut,' Aliyah said. 'Oh, and Edmund – fuck the English.'

Edmund smiled.

Tiffany squeezed Edmund's hand 'Wherever we land, we'll be together.'

Fortified by this, Edmund counted: 'One....Two...Three!' and together they leapt into the Anomaly.

'Frimmel,' Chase said, then checked himself. 'Hans. Am I still under arrest?'

Frimmel smiled. '... I will have to ask my superiors, Wiener.'

'Wiener?' Ronan echoed.

'Don't ask,' Chase dismissed.

'A word of advice, Sergeant,' Beth said. 'Keep an eye on those Nazis. They're bad news.'

Frimmel nodded understanding. Then he clicked to attention, saluted Chase and Ronan, who returned the salute sincerely. Frimmel then spun on his heel and marched into the Anomaly.

'Come on, Ronan,' Chase said as he took Beth's hand. 'It's time to go.'

'I'm not going,' Ronan told him.

'What?'

'I'm staying here, with Aliyah.'

Aliyah looked at the clasped hands. 'And it looks like you're leaving with Chase,' she said to Beth.

Beth released Chase's hand and approached Aliyah. 'You know how it is,' she said softly.

'Yeah, I know. But who am I gonna watch the new season of *Outlander* with?'

Beth looked across at Ronan. Ronan looked back confused. 'What's Outlander?'

'Ronan,' Chase interrupted. 'You can't stay. You don't belong here.'

'Does anyone really belong anywhere?'

'What is that supposed to mean?'

'I don't know,' Ronan admitted. 'It sounded better in my head.'

'We have to go back,' Chase insisted. 'We have to preserve the timeline.'

'No, we don't. If there's one thing we've learned through all this, it's that the timeline can take care of itself. And you're not going home anyway.'

'How do you know?' Chase challenged.

Ronan gestured to old Chase standing at the side of the field. Chase conceded the point. 'So I'm staying here with Aliyah, and you're going off with Beth to whenever, and neither of us are returning to 2100. Admit it. This is how it *has* to end. Otherwise,' again Ronan gestured to old Chase, 'you would not be here.'

'So, I guess that's it.'

'I guess that's it.'

'So long, partner.' Chase gave Ronan a heartfelt hug. They may have endangered, and then saved, the universe; but now that he was losing his best friend he wondered if it was all worth it. 'I'm gonna miss you.'

'I won't miss you,' Ronan told him. Chase pulled away. 'I've got your 'old man' self to keep me company.'

Chase smiled. Looked across at old Chase. He waved. 'Tell him to go fuck himself.'

Old Chase waved back. 'Fuck you!' he called out, then threw something at Chase the younger. Chase caught it with one hand – the Pod.

Chase laughed, wiped a tear from his face.

Beth gave Aliyah a hug, then took Chase by the hand. 'Come on, you. We're out of time.'

Ronan laughed. 'Ha!'

The Anomaly had shrunk to about 6-foot in diameter; in a few more seconds it could be gone forever. Beth dragged Chase after her into the bubble – and as the band finished the song, the Anomaly shrivelled into a singularity and *'popped'* out of existence. In its place a white rat suddenly appeared and fell to the ground.

'Felix!' Ronan cried. He picked up the rat, overjoyed to see it alive. 'Ah, Felix.'

As Ronan stroked Felix, old Chase finally approached.

'So where did you and Beth end up?' Ronan asked.

Old Chase smiled. 'The land of milk and honey. Xanadu and Shangri-la and Nirvana all rolled – '

' – Oh, all right. If you don't want to tell me just say so you cryptic old bastard. I preferred you when you were young and reckless.' He continues petting Felix, 'At least I have you, Felix.'

'Excuse me!' Aliyah punched Ronan in the shoulder. Hard.

'Ow! And you, my love. Of course. Meet Felix.' He held the rat up to her face.

Aliyah, unfazed, considered the rat for a moment. 'Why are its eyes pink?'

'He's albino.'

'Is it house trained?'

CHAPTER 18
And So It Begins

Beth and Chase emerged from the Anomaly just as it shrank into nothingness. They found themselves standing in a field on a bright sunny day.

'Where are we?' Beth asked. 'And *when* are we?'

'Guess.'

Beth looked around. They were not alone. There were hundreds of young people milling about or setting up tents. Thousands more were on the way. In the distance she could see an army of stagehands setting up a stage.

A voice came over the PA. 'Testing ... Testing. One TWO! One TWO!'

She realised they were on Max Yasgur's dairy farm in Bethel, New York. The day was August 14, 1969 – a Thursday. Woodstock was due to begin the following day.

'How did you know?'

'Aliyah told me.'

Beth threw her arms around Chase the younger and planted a kiss on his mouth. 'I'm looking forward to growing old with you, Chase Tomley.'

Meanwhile in Munich, November 9, 1923, Sergeant Frimmel was returned to Odeonsplatz square. It was night, several hours after he had left, and the square was surprisingly quiet and still. There was no evidence of the confrontation with the Nazi's earlier that day, assuming it had still happened; and the Hellgate had vanished behind him, leaving everything as it was.

Now that he was back it all seemed like a dream; but then he reached into his pocket and found Beth's iPhone. He had been filming their adventures with it and neglected to give it back to her. So … not a dream.

But had history been changed, or was it restored to the future Beth had warned him about? He thought of Ilsa and her family. They were Jewish. It hadn't really occurred to him before because it didn't matter. But now it did. Now his beloved Germany would turn against them. If so, that was a Fatherland he did not want to be a part of anymore. He would take his family, and Ilsa and her family, away from this place before it was too late. Perhaps to England, or America … or maybe Australia. He'd always wanted to see a kangaroo.

With a new found purpose Hans Frimmel ran out of the square to find Ilsa.

Meanwhile, out back of a York farmhouse in the year of our Lord 1086, on what was still a miserable, drizzly, Thursday afternoon, Edmund and Tiffany tumbled out of Doomsday Bubble and into the mud. Beside them were a pig sty and chicken coop, and at his feet was the Doomsday book, right where he had dropped it.

Edmund picked up the book.

'What's that?' Tiffany asked.

'Nothing important,' Edmund said, then threw the book into the pig sty.

Tiffany looked at the squalid farmhouse. 'Is this your home?' There was no judgement in her voice, though she did seem a bit disappointed.

'No. This is York. I live in London.' Edmund looked about the property and the neighbouring farms. The first time he walked these roads he had been head down and on a mission for the king. That mission no longer mattered, and the thought of returning to London filled him with dread. He now looked upon the squat little houses in a new light. They seemed charming to him. Even cosy. And the lush green countryside with its rolling hills covered in purple heather, and rows of Ash and Sycamore trees was positively glorious, despite (or perhaps because of) the gloomy weather. How had he not noticed this before? York was a beautiful part of the world.

'Are we going to London, then?' Tiffany asked.

Edmund had made his decision. 'This is our home now. You said your people came from here. Let's find them, shall we?'

Meanwhile, in New York City in the year 2018 – a Tuesday – Aliyah showed Ronan around her apartment. He carried Felix the rat, now tucked inside a cage they had found at Yankee Stadium (the cage was kept on hand for any stray animals – cats, squirrels, raccoons – that sometimes wandered onto the field during a game).

'It ain't much, but it's home.'

'It's great. Isn't it Felix?'

'I guess since Beth won't be coming back any time soon you can have her room. But this is strictly platonic, you understand.'

'Of course.' Ronan put Felix down, then moved in for a kiss.

'And the rat stays in the cage, otherwise the deal's off. End of discussion.'

'Absolutely.' Another kiss.

'And you'll have to get a job. Pay your share of the rent.'

'No problem.' Kiss.

'And probably my share too. At least for now.'

'No problem.' Kiss.

'Have you ever worked in the theatre?'

'No. But I can learn.' Kiss.

'Flatmates. That's all.'

'Strictly platonic.' This time the kiss stuck.

Aliyah stopped talking and wrapped her arms around him. That accent was to die for.

Meanwhile, elsewhere in New York City in the year 2018, old Chase entered his motel room, turned on the TV, and began packing his meagre belongings into a sports bag.

The news was on. ' – Again, just recapping. It seems the wormhole that was consuming New York city has just disappeared. Shrunk out of existence. We're getting various reports that it had something to do with all the historical visitors singing show-tunes at it in Yankee Stadium. Now, I find that very hard to believe, frankly; but stranger things have happened. Meanwhile President Trump has thanked the army for its role in eradicating the wormhole and getting rid of the illegal immigrants that had been pouring into the country because of it, calling it a *tremendous achievement* for his administration…'

Chase picked up a framed photo from the bedside table. It was of himself and Beth, middle-aged and happy, living in suburban Connecticut in the 1980s. They had run a tech business together and had done quite well for themselves, with hundreds of patents to their name, having been key players in the digital revolution of the 1970s.

But that was a long time ago now, and Beth did not live long into the 90's. Cancer.

Chase packed the photo in the sports bag and zipped it up.

Meanwhile, in the Fellows' dining room of Gonville & Caius College of Cambridge University, in the year 2009, Sunday June 28th, the grandfather clock chimed the hour – 3:00 pm.

Professor Steven Hawking sat in his wheelchair alone in the Hall. It had been three hours, and no-one had come to his Time Travellers Reception.

'Professor Hawking? It's three o'clock,' the head waiter said.

Hawking responded via his voice-box, 'I guess no-one is coming. It seems time travel isn't possible, after all. Pity.'

As Hawking exited the room, the waiter turned out the lights, leaving all the wonderful food to spoil in the dark – or at least until the servers returned to clean up and donate it to the local Food Bank.

Fifteen minutes later someone came running up the stairs to the dining room. The lights flicked on, and a not quite so old Chase entered, puffing and out of breath. He looked about the empty room. 'Damn. I missed it!' Unfortunately, his plane had been delayed due to unexpected bad weather.

Chase shrugged, sat down, and raised a flute of ready-poured champagne. 'This one's for you, Ronan.'

But before he could bring the glass to his lips a blinding flash of light exploded in the middle of the room, and Felix the rat dropped out of thin air onto a tray of canapes. Chase picked up the rat and gave it an affectionate stroke with his finger. Then Felix disappeared from his hand – returned to the future.

'And so it begins.'

Phil Moore is a Filmmaker, Author, Composer and Teacher. He lives in Sydney, Australia.

Other books by Phil include:

- *Return of the Prophet* , and its companion book *Shentama*
- *Terra Utopia*

and the Filmmaking Reference work —

- *Fuck Art, Just Tell the Story*

All of which you will find wherever good Books are sold.

You can find out more about Phil and his various creative efforts at **philmoore.net**

www.ingramcontent.com/pod-product-compliance
Lightning Source LLC
Chambersburg PA
CBHW072054170626
46813CB00004B/1341